Talon

Talon

A Novel of Suspense

James Coltrane

THE BOBBS-MERRILL COMPANY, INC.

Indianapolis / New York

Designed by Gail Herzog Conwell

Manufactured in the United States of America

First printing

Library of Congress Cataloging in Publication Data

Coltrane, James.
    Talon: a novel of suspense.

    I. Title.
PZ4.C7256Tal   [PS3553.04775]   813'.5'4   77-15436
ISBN 0-672-52391-4

To Fred, Kristin, Jenifer,
and the children of my dreams

PRELUDE

Sunday, July 4, 1971

In 1971 the Soviet Union produced 800 thousand tons of copper ore, Australia grazed better than 164 million sheep, and Liberia had 27 million gross tons of ships plying the waters of the world, principally under flags of convenience. The United States sawed through 40 million tons of logs for wood pulp, a disproportionate share of which, in the form of paper, wound up in Washington, D.C.

The principal repository for the United States intelligence community's vast pile of information is a blank-walled reinforced-concrete building located off Columbia Park.

Most of the work taking place at the super-secret National Reconnaissance Office's data center consists of reducing the gathered intelligence information to a form which can be made accessible to community analysts by computer. At the N.R.O., mountains of paper become electronic signals on magnetic tape. Incoming data from spies, books, newspapers, periodicals, satellites, submarines, sona-buoys and the like are collated, transcribed and cataloged. The building is full of energy and the genius of man.

All statistics on the historical worldwide production of copper, ship bottoms and paper, on sheep, weather and people, as well as every other available almanac-type fact, take up a few cubic feet of space in one of this building's low-level computers. The high-level intelligence information on paper, microfiche and computer tape fills to overflowing the rest of the N.R.O.'s nine acres of floor space.

The wonder is that, on that holiday weekend, the building did not pulsate, that it did not keen in the summer heat, warp itself and its eight levels of subbasements free from their underpinnings in the mere earth and sweep into orbit, trailing its tendrils of connections to humankind.

The windowless monolith, replete with the knowledge of the world in dollars and kopeks, barrels and casks, flesh and crops, guns and butter, instead, slept in the July heat and Potomac humidity. The sleeping cement giant was unaware of and ill-prepared for the spider on its hide.

It's hard to breathe in Washington's summer. Oppressive. The air shifts. But not so that you can identify the movement as a breeze. What air movement there was on that Fourth of July Sunday carried the occasional sound of fireworks.

Drops of sweat hit the concrete walkway at the rear alley of the N.R.O. building. The source was a man suspended, spread-eagled and motionless, from a web of three-hundred-pound-test fishing-line leader, halfway up the eighty-foot sheer wall. Each filament of leader had a mountain climber's D-ring on the end. Each D-ring was snapped to a link, which was in turn fastened to a bolt that the man had shot into the wall, starting at street level.

He was resting. For fifteen minutes he remained motionless; then he started the climb again. He used a Hilti-gun, a standard construction tool. It had been stolen to order and then modified to reduce the report produced by the .22-caliber blank cartridges that fired the anchor bolts into the solid concrete. At each of ninety-odd points in the wall so far, he had fired the Hilti and firmly secured a link with a wing nut. Then he had snapped the D-ring from the lowest line on his web to the new link. Then he edged his foot, shod with a steel-soled moto-cross boot, up to the next protruding bolt, gaining six inches. Finally he removed the nut and link from the point he had just unsnapped, leaving only the bolt showing. After every ten shots he replaced the magazine of the Hilti.

It was arduous. The climb took nearly two hours. He was soaked with perspiration when he rolled over the parapet and onto the roof. He lay still and rested.

He was a slight figure, huddled there on the roof. He wore a light-weight standard-issue U.S. Air Force flight suit manufactured by Berger Brothers Company in 1959, one of millions made. He had never broken a bone, never had a tooth filled. He looked faintly Oriental in build and coloring, enough so that he might have been one of those combinations of ingredients the tourist to Hawaii adores, but not so much that anyone would have given him a second look in passing.

He stirred. Reaching into a pocket at his left calf, he pulled out a nylon bag. He packed his web into it. Then he tied the bag to the end of a quarter-inch nylon rope with which he would later rappel down the side of the building. Using the Hilti, he shot a bolt into the inside of the parapet. He fastened a link onto it. Then he looped the nylon rope through a D-ring and snapped it to the tie-down point.

He unzipped the cigarette pocket on the left shoulder of the flight suit and took out a one-ounce ball of C-4, a plastic explosive. He molded it around the base of the bolt. He took a standard-issue U.S. Government M1 time-delay detonator from the left shoulder pencil pocket and pushed it into the explosive. Perfect. He watched for kinks as he carefully coiled the rope on the roof, under the tie-down point. Then he snapped the Hilti to his belt and crawled to the elevator stack, where he lay still in the shadows for a few minutes.

He unbuckled the leather climbing harness from under his arms and refastened it at his waist. A bag containing a computer tape swung heavily at his side. He took a towel from his right calf pocket and dried his face. Then he

3

unzipped the front of the flight suit and wiped his body. He folded the towel, placed it beneath his head, and slept.

Three hours later, at eight-fifteen, he awoke. The sun was down. The air was cooler, the humidity higher. There were thunder claps and flashes of lightning to the north, over Bethesda and Chevy Chase. Good. Thunder was as good as the Fourth itself to cover the explosion of the plastic, which would free up the bolt and allow him to recover the rope and shackle—the only obvious traces of his entry. It would leave only a small pockmark in the parapet. The bolts would hardly be noticeable on the textured finish of the exterior wall.

He placed the towel in his pocket and stretched, working out climbing kinks and cramps. He removed a small flashlight from his right breast pocket. He felt around the steel fire door. Wisps of refrigerated air escaping at the edges made him ache to get in. The hinges were outside. He tapped out the pins with a small hammer and a drift from the electrician's tool kit hung on his belt. The door was heavy. With a screwdriver, he slowly edged it off the hinges. He checked with a dentist's mirror for an alarm as soon as he had space. Then he pulled the door open a little more. It stayed on the jamb, so he was able to squeeze in without dropping the door. The cold air inside was marvelous.

Eighty-eight dollars and twenty cents paid by the N.R.O. had secured the purchase and installation of a Detex exit-control lock. From the inside, roof access could be gained only by key or by pressing a paddle marked EMERGENCY EXIT ONLY and PUSH HERE, ALARM WILL SOUND. The spider chuckled. The alarm was on the wrong side of the door.

He replaced the flashlight in its pocket. Uncle had plenty of money. The lights were on twenty-four hours a day. He unscrewed the bulb just inside the door, to keep light from spilling onto the roof. The thunderstorm had moved into Arlington now, and it was pouring outside.

4

He relieved himself at the top-floor landing. He started down the stairs. Conveniently marked. No closed-circuit TV. He stopped at each landing and looked around the corner with the dentist's mirror. He found the only checkpoint at the first floor.

The entrance guard booth extended back to the stairs, and a safety-glass window provided control. After watching for several minutes, the spider decided the booth was empty. He kept low, slipped past, and was about to check the next flight when he heard footsteps and wheezing coming up. Adrenaline started booming through his veins. Breathing hard and shaking, he unhooked the Hilti from his belt. His heart was throbbing, and a mule was kicking his gut.

He pushed the muzzle of the Hilti into an olive-green chest as it came around the corner. He pulled the trigger. There was a pop, a surprised pair of eyes, and the guard fell back. The spider was ready to run for the roof. But there wasn't a sound except the pounding in his ears. He looked around the corner. No movement from the tumbled heap at the bottom of the stairs.

He went down and looked at the body. There was a small bloody spot in the uniform at heart level, where the bolt had gone in. The guard was dead.

He stepped over the corpse and continued down the stairs until he came to sublevel four. He opened the door and stepped into the brightly lit computer area. Time had now become critical. He cursed when he found the data bank in use. Precious seconds disappeared. Ruhr coal-production figures for 1967 were being transmitted to the Bonn branch of the Office of Naval Intelligence.

The spider fumed while the big magnetic tape reels jiggled back and forth. Finally movement stopped. He pressed the fast-rewind button. Then he opened the glass front and removed the tape. He took a similar reel of magnetic tape from the bag at his side. He checked the gummed label to make sure it was identical to the original. He threaded on his substitute.

Time was crashing by him. He closed the computer. He unzipped a pocket and took out a magnet. He removed the label from the old reel. Then he put it on a table, ran the magnet over it, and placed it among a large number of blank computer tapes on a shelf. Done. He raced for the steps.

He gained the upper levels, not pausing at the guard's body. Two floors from the roof he stopped, checked his thinking, and listened for alarms. He was still holding the magnet. He replaced it in the correct pocket. He ran up the final flights to the roof landing.

He glanced at his watch. Twenty-two minutes since he'd entered the building. He was sweating again.

He screwed the bulb back in at the top landing and squeezed outside. Using his screwdriver, he levered the door back onto its hinges. He tapped the hinge pins home. He used the flashlight to check the hinges, then dropped it back into the right breast pocket. He zipped everything up. He walked to the roof edge, picked up the nylon line and threw it over. He set up for rappeling. He sat on the parapet wall, then reached down to his shackle point and armed the M1 detonator by crushing its ampule of acid. It would take about three minutes for the acid to eat through a wire and trip the firing device.

He slipped over the roof edge, worked down about nine feet and planted his feet against the wall. He pushed out and slacked off the line for a short, controlled fall, the friction of the line around his body slowing the pull of gravity. Twenty feet from the rooftop he set up for another push outward, this time for a long fall. He swung out and started slipping the line. Ten feet into the fall, a crimp in the nylon rope hung up in the shackle, and the line stopped slipping. The sudden catch turned him upside down. His suddenly short line swung him back, smashing his head against the wall. Then he was hanging upside down, forty feet from the back-alley sidewalk. Stunned.

He shook his head. He was thirsty. Blood was dripping from his head. His harness had slipped to his hips. He shook his head again and reached up to the rope, straining to get right side up. It was still drizzling, and hot. He was soaked with sweat and rain. He tore his elbow and knee on the studs he'd shot into the wall earlier.

He was slow. He had too many things hanging on him to allow him easy movement. Alarms started going off in the building.

The dead guard's friend at the central-security switchboard had hesitated nearly ten minutes after the mandatory check-in time before raising a hue and cry. After all, nothing had happened in eight and a half years.

The spider was now upright and climbing. He had to free the crimp in the rope. He wondered how much time had gone by. If he could clear it, it would take him only a few seconds to rappel down. As he reached over the parapet wall, the M1 went off, triggering the plastic and blasting the tie-down bolt out of the wall. It took him less than a second and a half to make it to the sidewalk, free-fall.

1

"Woof," he said, playfully placing a hand on the girl's thigh.

"Huh?"

"Woof!" he repeated.

"What're ya doin'?" Her eyes started to glaze. This was New York, and here she was alone in this guy's apartment. She tried to move over.

"Woof, woof!" he said, this time leaning over for a kiss.

She reached out to defend herself with all the aplomb a Prudential receptionist from the Bronx could muster, and removed a silverfish-sized chunk of meat from Joe Talon's cheek.

"Eek!" she said. Now she'd done it. Swiftly she jumped from the couch, grabbed her pocketbook and coat, and was gone. The blood had barely started to well up under Talon's blue left eye when the door slammed.

"Damn!" he said. "Damn every goddamn Bronx insurance company receptionist," he said as he reached behind the couch for a Kleenex. "No sense of humor in this goddamn town." Holding a ball of tissue to his face, he walked into the bathroom and looked at himself in the mirror out of his brown right eye.

It was a nation of sheep, he thought, but why did he always end up with Black Bart's girl?

With a tire-patch-sized Band-Aid stemming the red tide, he walked into the kitchen. He used his martial-arts training in Aikido to good advantage in suppressing a scream as he came toe-to-toe with a chair leg, and lost on the exchange. It was one of those nights.

Ah, Talon, he thought, as he cracked a big bottle of Foster beer. He figured he'd done all right even to think two words after spending a very liquid Thursday night at Friday's, falling in lust with Godzilla's aunt, and then her escaping his clutches with probably only an ounce of his flesh under her fingernail. Ah, Talon, what a simple life you lead. A schizoid's delight. The Department of Agriculture. Only thirty-seven and able to spout "Hereford" and "mulch" like an aggie.

He remembered that he'd forgotten his evening meditation and decided it was too late to recoup the lost opportunity to gain rest and strength. He got after the rest of the Foster beer.

New York was the best of places and the worst of places. He thought of his attempts to bring Southern California to the land of the midnight mugging, and he felt depressed. He walked into the living room and kicked a tire from his Beezer. The rest of the motorcycle had been languishing for some months in a garage, awaiting the decision on whether to chop or sell.

He fantasized a chop: rebored engine with new pistons, a rake to the triple-tree, front fork extension, hard tail, and sissy bar. The B.S.A. would shine with chrome and custom hand-rubbed lacquer, and his cult of the West finally might come to be. The infection would spread over New York, and California Dreamin' would become a reality.

He put a Beach Boys record on his stereo and slouched on the couch while "Little Deuce Coupe" shattered through the two A.M. stillness at 48 West Seventy-fifth Street.

In his mind—or head, as the Californian in him would prefer to refer to the vehicle for thinking—he knew that the Beezer was as much a relic as his ten-foot Surfboards Hawaii semi-gun which temporarily was hanging over the fireplace. The wax now streaked down the glassy surface, and drip marks on the floor were a reminder of the few opportunities he'd had to actually light the logs in the wood-burning fireplace as a means of levering some recalcitrant fluff into the bedroom. There was a big difference between Waimea and Sheepshead, as bays went. His gun had hung there temporarily for seven years now, not counting two years of storage in D.C., before his transfer to the Big Apple.

The record changer did its job. Ian and Sylvia harmonized on "Early Morning Rain." Talon started thinking about 1966 and realized the Beezer had to go. If it didn't, and he chopped that old horse, the hard tail would kill his kidneys.

His rising sign was Libra. Maybe a middle-of-the-road solution? He was appalled at himself as he picked his way through the carnage of his bedclothes and burped into the bathroom. The heartbreak of psoriasis and the pain of being Gemini. Let it get stolen and collect the insurance, or fix it stock and customize it next year? He considered the implications.

He was wracked with ambivalence in trying to decide. He finished brushing his teeth. He took a shower. He made a decision. He'd have Ghost Motorcycles from Port Washington pick up his scooter tomorrow. He'd get all six hundred and fifty cubic centimeters in order and wait for a promotion. Then he'd reward himself with a custom job.

With this decision made, he fell on his couch, which still smelled like Laverne, and passed out. Tom Rush was singing about "Do Re Mi" and the problems the Okies had had in gaining access to California. A car in the street outside was still lying in wait for the Friday alternate side. A little snow, caked with airborne and canine debris, melted in the gutter as winter interfaced with the ides of March.

2

"Hello, motha . . . ," a down-home black voice drawled out of a Panasonic digital alarm clock-radio in the bedroom. Talon moaned and missed most of the Yoo Hoo commercial. He was not surprised to hear it was Yogi Berra's favorite drink. Friday. Talon sat up on the couch and started trying to get ready for the day. He tried to open his eyes. The right one worked. The left felt as though someone had dropped epoxy on it. He'd forgotten to take out his left contact lens in the morning stupor.

He walked into the bathroom, with the sensation of the Seven Santini Brothers moving a piano around in the back of his head. The mirror didn't help his disposition, but he managed to pry open his left eye and pop out the brown contact lens. Two nearsighted blue eyes stared back at him from across the sink. He turned on the porcelain-handled cold-water tap and went to the kitchen to find a cigarette.

The sound of rushing water calmed his throbbing pulse as the nicotine started to work. He smoked sparingly, but with a chewy bat-cavern mouth that first Kool, the morning after the night before—that was dynamite.

Seven years in New York and no California girls, no simplicity, lots of excess adipose. While he showered, he remembered working Cannons down at Hermosa Beach two lives ago. That day it was running a real five or six feet, his timing was on, and he sizzled across the faces of the waves, his head dipping in the fast curls, kicking out at the optimum moment and feeling fine about being nineteen.

Dangerous, he thought, as he peed in the shower. Chicks

12

always freaked out when he did that. Dangerous to go back to those halcyon days. Life was more than living in a van; rolling around with a simple, oh wow, sun-blond pearl-toothed moose; listening for the surf reports. He put the contacts back in and shaved.

It had been six months and a lot of miles under the sheets since his last mama had moved on. The schizoid-career thing wrought havoc on anything long-term. Maybe it's me, he thought, as he dragged on his pants. And his work-bred suspicions of anyone who was not of his other world. He put on a flower-print shirt and a crew-neck sweater. He put on the leather jacket he had bought in Munich when he was freezing his rear there in 1968. He set an impressive anti-burglar bar in the floor and slid it home as he stepped out the door.

He was walking down the stairs to the I.N.D., the Museum of Natural History lowering above him, when he remembered that he'd forgotten his morning meditation. He wondered whether the Maharishi marked the falling of a leaf. Well, he'd try it standing up.

He stood in the midst of the subway crowd, strap-hanging. The car swayed. He closed his eyes, relaxed, and started the mantra. Droning away, he repeated the meaningless word over and over. Thoughts came, but, as instructed by a fresh-washed, clean-shaven mentor two months before, he innocently preferred the secret syllables designed to aid him in transcending.

"What are you doing?" a voice came probing at him through the mist of his meditation.

"Huh?"

"You're not fooling me at all. You're not asleep. You're rubbing on me, you pervert!"

He tried to think. He was still on the train, it was crowded, and someone over his left shoulder was poking at him.

"If you don't quit it, I'm going to poke you!"

He noticed an impressive-looking umbrella point being

brandished under his chin. Meditation was no fun when interrupted like this. He tried to explain. "I'm ..."

"I'm going to scream if you don't quit."

Even on the subway, people will look if the action seems appealing enough. They were looking. He tried to turn to get a handle on the situation and nearly had a contact lens removed by an erect *New York Times*. "Look," he started to answer, and then fell silent. In awe.

He was a multimillion-mile public transportation club member. Never had he seen anything like what was looking up from a fur-fringed camel-hair coat. He froze.

"Quit trying to turn and stop your rubbing on me!"

It was the movement of the car. They just do that, lady, and the passengers move. He wanted to say it. He couldn't spit it out. Her dark blond hair disappeared over her back in a cascade. No makeup. Gold-flecked amber eyes. Maybe five foot seven. He prayed she had lousy legs. If she had lousy legs he could start breathing again. It was too crowded to see. The train kept up its sensual sway. "Uh ..." he said.

Her cheeks were really fired up now. As he raised an arm to protect his battle-scarred face, the umbrella point caught and removed his Band-Aid. Her beautiful mouth opened along with her nostrils and eyes in preparation for the coup de grâce. His elbow had touched a breast.

The expected scream, however, failed to materialize. Instead, a reasonably stilted voice expressed some concern over the wound in his cheek. The crowd had shifted, was thinner now, and he was no longer pressing against her.

"Are you sick or drunk?" she asked. Then the milk of human kindness curdled. "If you're drunk, I'm going to call a cop."

The train ground to a halt at Thirty-fourth Street. As the passengers cleared out, he managed a heavy-lidded squint at her legs. Never send to know for whom the bell tolls, he thought; it tolls for me. He was sure. No stockings; long, tan legs. Legs. He wanted to close his eyes and start the mantra going again.

Her hair was judiciously draped over her shoulders, and he wondered how the Nefertiti neck could support the weight of it and keep her chin raked up at ten degrees above the horizontal at the same time. He was about to comment on this when the door hissed shut, the train lurched and she bumped into him. Hard. Her umbrella grazed his wounded cheek. He felt like d'Artagnan.

She started sobbing, and he reached for her shoulder with one hand and an upright pole with the other as the train squealed and lurched. She put her head against his chest and dug the umbrella into his instep, and he fell in love.

At the next stop he guided her out the door and sat with her on a bench as the train left and her motor ran down.

"You've got my jacket damp," he said.

She started sobbing again. Brilliant, Talon, he thought. "I was only trying to add a bit of levity to a dismal day," he said.

Between the sobs he thought he heard, "I'm sorry about your cheek," and "Leave me alone," and "I'll scream if you don't." He wasn't positive, and she didn't move her head from his chest, so he just sat.

"Is everything all right?"

Talon looked up, seeing in rapid order black shoes, blues, gold buttons and a badge.

"Right, officer. She had a nasty fall, but it'll be fine."

She waved her hand noncommittally, after which the cop left and they settled into the subway noise and togetherness. Talon was getting concerned.

He managed to dislodge his wallet from his hip pocket and flip it open to his plastic Department of Agriculture I.D. He held it in front of her face.

"Look, I work for Agriculture, and I was just moving with the crowd. I couldn't really explain in there. I mean, what

15

would you do if *you* were meditating and minding your own business and someone started to raise hell with you?"

"You don't look that old."

"The product of an easy youth casting about the beaches of L.A. in search of the perfect wave and the endless summer."

"I don't like blond men."

"I don't like Cybill Shepherd, Grace Kelly or Karen Valentine. I don't know them. But I might want to. Why don't we start from there and work backward?"

"Your cheek looks like an eagle landed on it. I'm sorry."

"Shaving. Could be worse," he said. Liar, he thought.

"This is New York; I was scared."

"It's nothing. Look, let's find a Chock Full o' Nuts, get a cuppa, and relax."

"Why?"

"Why not?"

"I've been crying; I look terrible."

Like dust on the Mona Lisa. He could feel her warming. It was impossible. He'd better give up. No one could hassle this lady and live.

"Okay," she said, lifting her head from his chest.

"Huh?"

"Let's get some coffee."

"Sure."

"Tell me about agriculture." They got up and walked toward the exit.

"Later. Where are you from?"

"Lanikai, Oahu, Hawaii."

He perked right up. "Really? I surfed Waimea Bay once. The big ones . . . ."

"I bet it was a long time ago. You had one of those big long guns that weighed about forty pounds, huh?"

She was a witch. He made a mental note to store his board. Call the super right away. Store it and clean up the wax. He deflated. "Yeah, right."

"I didn't mean to hurt your feelings."

16

"No one gets his feelings hurt if he doesn't want to. But thanks, you're nice."

"You're nice, too."

Impossible. He looked out of the corner of his eye. She was real. No ectoplasm. He stuck a finger into her side. She jumped and looked suspicious.

"What's that for?" she quavered.

"I wanted to see if you were real."

"I am."

He found a White Rose Bar, and they ordered coffee at the rail. He didn't know where he was. Out of character for his training. "I thought you sounded different."

She laughed a throaty laugh. He wanted to bite her. "That's the Hawaiian."

"I thought so." The coffee scalded his throat. He never drank coffee. He was really nervous. He started thinking about a cigarette. He figured he'd refrain from bad habits.

"Smoke?" she said. She pulled a pack of Kools out of a needlepoint pocketbook and offered it.

Witch, he thought. "Sure," he said.

He lit up and looked at his watch. Nine-fifteen. He had to call in soon; otherwise there'd be a security flap.

"Do you have to go?" she said, looking at him and cocking her head to the side. The glare from her teeth was unbearable.

"No, I've got to call in sick."

"I can't spend too much time with you."

"Oh. Where were you going?"

"I've got to go down to the H.V.B.—Hawaii Visitors' Bureau office. Down at the Trade Center somewhere."

"Oh, you're a turista." He tried to say it gaily, but it fell flat. She'd come into his life like Kahoutek, and now she was leaving.

"I'm not leaving New York. I did some promotional work for H.V.B.; that's why I came to New York. And I'm sort of out of work—and money—so I thought I'd check in with them."

17

"How old are you?"

"Twenty-two."

He'd had her pegged a bit to the west of eighteen, but New York does funny things to people. "Will you have dinner with me?"

"When?"

"For the next year or two?" The throaty laugh again. His stomach went funny. He wanted the bartender to turn up the heat so he could see what was under the coat. But, at fifty cents a shot, the energy crisis was biting into the comfort of the White Rose regulars. He wanted to lean forward and kiss her. She was leaning forward. He did and she did. He almost fell off the stool. No open mouth, no tongue, no lipstick. Only heaven. He was in awe.

"Can we start with tonight?" she asked.

"Seven." He reached in his pocket and pulled out a twenty. He pressed it into a cool, dry palm. "Take a cab." He grabbed a napkin and borrowed a pen from the bartender. "Here's the address." He was close to tears. "Seven," he said again.

"Seven."

"Seven."

"I know, you already said that. What's your brand, Mr. Aggie?"

"Joe Talon. What's yours?"

"Carlee Desha. It's French." She spelled it. "But pronounce it dee-shay."

"Okay. Seven."

"Right. I've got it."

"I just wanted to make sure," he said.

She reached over and squeezed his hand. No woman squeezing anywhere else had ever produced results like that. "See you tonight," she said.

"Right."

He levitated out of the bar and into a cab and made it down to 26 Federal Plaza. Late.

3

The door outside said "World Food Production—Research Division." "Morning, Moneypenny," Talon said as he bobbled into the reception area. He always said good morning like that. She, Pauli D'Arcy, always sniffed at him from behind her plush chest. Today, no sniff. Today she popped his bubble.

"There's an inquiry out for you. That's the second this year."

"One more point and I lose my license, right?"

"Mr. Talon." She heaved her bosom forward confidentially and rested it on the desk. Lucky no one uses inkwells anymore, he thought. "Your ass is in a sling. Mr. Flynn *already* has a pro crew flying up from Langley."

"Keep them on their toes, eh, Moneypenny? What are the pros for, after all?"

She pressed a button under her desk and gave Talon access to a door marked "Reading Room." He ignored her snort and walked through.

He felt put upon. He was only forty minutes late. He was in love. He had not, as far as he knew, come up with anything concrete in nine years at this job. So how could they worry about him? He didn't know anything. Through the door. Through the looking glass. His mind did a one-eighty. He shed the cow manure and corn.

His hand and resolve were firm as he opened Flynn's door. Screw 'em, he thought.

"Come in, Joe."

"Morning, M."

"Talon, if you don't cut that out, you'll be out."

"It's my only chance to laugh. Ha, ha."

"We're going to have to screen you again."

Standard operating procedure after his forty-minute defection. He was going to be taped and wired and cross-examined again. The pro crew would have the gear with them. "Fine," he said. Screw 'em, he thought.

"You'll never get anywhere if you keep this up."

"I'll never get anywhere because I'm from California. Jack, you're the only Episcopal Flynn in the Manhattan directory. Everyone knows the Company is a stand-up East Coast WASP's nest."

Flynn managed a sigh. He surveyed Talon's outfit, which was in accordance with the book, but garish. "You've got some kind of flower . . ."

"It's called an aloha shirt."

"How's your memory?"

"You know better than me, Jack. You've got it all; you own it."

"Cut the bitter stuff, Joe. This is no glory game. This is no ego builder for us."

Talon's mind short-circuited. It was a great facility. His answer to sermons, lectures and drivel. Nod and adopt an air of watchful waiting. Pretty soon the gas gives out.

A knock interrupted. Rather, two. In walked Miss D'Arcy.

"The team is here," she said.

Talon turned to follow her. He heard Jack Flynn's last words, ". . . quit calling her Moneypenny and get on Sanroc."

Flynn is basically a nice guy, Talon thought. Pretty much. If a guy wears only two suits in the seven years he's been your boss, he's got to be a nice guy. He had been some kind of clerk in Donovan's army, the old OSS. Now he managed a quiet, reputable corner of the multifaceted Central Intelligence Agency.

Talon didn't really know what Flynn did. He didn't know what any of the forty or fifty other clerks in his section did. He could only guess. The Company wasn't big on clucking coffee breaks. Simple covers, lots of farm stories for cocktail parties, plausible patter for wives, girlfriends, children, and the more important people in the world, two of whom he was going to play word games with right now.

From the beginning it was fluky. Maybe it was Vietnam fever and Kennedyitis. Talon knew he never should have been recruited, even on a contract basis. The Company was not some college trying to achieve geographical balance and racial parity. It was pure Ivy. He was sure the roaches in the men's room had gone to Harvard.

But he loved it. The Gemini in him dug the need to maintain two lives. He was being paid to be Walter Mitty.

But he hated it. He wanted a permanent assignment with real training. All he did now was lend-lease thinking. He was resourceful, creative and hard. He had a steel-trap memory. He was also a wild pain in the ass, wanted more money, smoked the occasional joint, and was too goddamn imaginative. Add the chance of a resurgence of his L.A. blood and the liberal lineage therein, and he was practically Che in the midst of the establishment.

He waited outside the I room. Interview or interrogation: it depended on your point of view. He held the latter, so maybe they were right. Whoever they were. Maybe he didn't fit.

He tensed up his gut and conjured up anxiety. Shallow breathing and eye squints. He pulled up shivers from his crotch and bounced them off his spine. He was getting ready for a try at lying.

He thought he had the way to beat the polygraph. He'd done a lot of reading and thinking about it. He knew it could be done. Maybe this time he'd try.

21

They called him in and attached the gear. They were scary. Talon wanted to bust the big one in the blue suit, who gave a sneering look at his shirt. Screw 'em, he thought. He started to run through the physiological ploys as the questions started. On top of it all he repeated to himself: she won't be there tonight. That really made him want to cry.

He did something he'd never done before. He lied and pulled it off. Subtle questions, subtle lies. He succeeded, too. In the past, when the answers had been wrong, they'd requestioned him. The answers he twisted this time went smooth as silk.

Of course, he didn't lie about the homosexual questions. He avoided the questions about the morning, and success-fully defended the dialogue with the pros which had preceded the polygraph connection.

"What happened this morning?" one had asked. He was younger, wore a gray suit, and had a deep drawl. Oil money in the family, Talon would have bet.

"I had a hangover from last night. I stopped to get some coffee and just didn't feel like moving."

"Why no call?" Blue asked.

"I was too hung over."

"Did you meet anyone?" Gray asked.

"No." Unhesitatingly. None of their business.

And so it had gone in dialogue. Then they hooked him up and tried to rip him with his yes-and-no answers. They got nothing. Nothing about him and the girl.

He wanted to tell them how good he was, how ready he was, how he could hold out in questioning. No way.

After they finished with him he left, and other Company personnel started filing in. Talon figured they were making something out of the trip.

In one respect, his section was a terrible pain in the ass, he thought. Fifteen minutes AWOL and the world goes wild. They call out the horse marines for a fart. But it was interesting. In any event, he was sick of being wetback contract labor. He wanted a position.

He was just sitting down in his carrel when the phone rang.

"Mr. Talon. This is Ms. D'Arcy. Mr. Flynn wants to see you again?"

"Right," he said. Why do they always have to end with a question? Screw 'er.

He got depressed sitting there trying to get up the energy to get back into the administrative fray. He looked at his carrel. It was a nine-by-ten room with a large work desk, a primary computer, reference books, a teletype for communication and a computer tie to Company headquarters at Langley, Virginia, and through the Company computer to the vast data banks at the National Reconnaissance Office in Washington. He could also tie into Goddard Space Flight Center in Maryland. There was lots of sophisticated photo-analysis gear. Stereo-sight gear. Distance analyzers. No windows.

He was tired. It was partly the hangover, partly that he wanted to be doing something exciting. He got out a cigarette and lit it. Be a draftsman, the matchbook said. Shit, he practically was. For years he'd been just a mechanic with the Company. Two years of training to read Computer Photo Remakes—C.P.R.s—in Washington, D.C. And then seven years—seven effing years—in New York looking at them—oil and whales, troops and planes, crop failures and floods—checking the C.P.R. satellite pictures until it seemed he knew every mountain in Afghanistan, every field in Montana.

In a periodic sweep taking nine days, two Sanrocs, the ultrasophisticated Space Analysis and Radio Orbiting Computers, observe and record the surface of the earth in ten-mile-square increments. A Sanroc, using a shift-scan high-resolution telescope, converts each one-hundred-square-mile earth image into twenty-five billion pixels, or elements of reflected and generated light intensity. Each pixel is broken down further to the seven basic spectrum colors and four infrared bands. Each of the eleven bands is then split into 128 gradations of lightness. Each resulting increment of value in the image is then given a numerical matrix assignment and stored, along with the information gathered on all other sections of the earth, for telemetric transmittal to earth for computer reassembly.

Then to analysis. First, by computer for aberrational comparisons against established norms for each earth section, dating back to work done before 1972. If the computer finds an aberration, it spits out a C.P.R. for human review. The computer identifies new sources of infrared, sweep-band radiation, and color-phase shifts, as well as geological, meteorological and man-induced changes in the world. These help identify a myriad of natural and man-made phenomena.

The importance to the intelligence gatherers of the Army, Navy, Air Force, and C.I.A.—the "community"—is tremendous. Millions upon millions of images are matched up against norms—the binary system matching numerical indices faster and more accurately than a million Talons looking at photos.

Only aberrations, changes from the computer's stored norms, trigger a human view. Simple. When an aberration showed, the earth section would be reproduced as a C.P.R., sent to analysis, and studied. Talon owned half a million square miles of India and Red China. It had been his domain for a month. Forty-two of Talon's five thousand earth sectors or quadrants lay on his table for aberration analysis this week. Before that he had had part of South America. Boring.

Other spy satellites use other methods, from simple photographs to radar scan. But Sanroc, from its inception, has been the most advanced and the most foolproof primary means of satellite surveillance. Sanroc uses radio telemetry to transmit the information in electronic bleeps to a ground station.

The nine-day Sanroc cycle fit in well with Talon's routine. He generally finished his reports well before the end of the cycle. It gave him some time to think.

Flynn, Talon thought. Fifteen minutes had gone by since the Company's Valkyrie had knocked. Talon wrote himself a note to call about his scooter and surfboard, pushed away from his work table, and went to see what was cooking.

4

"Not bad, Joe."

"Thanks, M."

Flynn looked up from the polygraph tabulations and started to change color. "I told you to cut that M stuff out, Talon. It makes for discipline problems here . . ."

"Right. You let me do it and everyone'll want to."

"Look, I'm doing the best I can. You've got the qualifications. It's your goddamn attitude, Joe. I understand you, but you piss people off. Anyway, that was the best personal interview you've had."

Personal interview, my ass. With wires connected to my mind, Talon thought.

"They were asking about your sudden . . ." Flynn groped.

"Adjustment?"

"Better adjustment."

"Strictly a matter of maturity."

"Very funny. Anyone else, no problem. You, and it's a problem. Why the change?"

"I'm getting more."

"That's enough of that. Seriously."

"I guess I'm trying to make amends. A permanent situation here." He tried to look contrite.

"Good, good. I hope it comes soon."

"Anything else?"

"That's all, Joe. Stay clean." Flynn paused. "By the way, Joe. No more M?"

"Okay. By the way, Jack . . ."

Flynn was looking down at his desk, through with him. "Yes?"

Talon waited until he looked up. "Up the Company," he said, turned his back, and left.

Flynn looked resigned as he went back to his administration.

Talon walked to his carrel. It was one-fifteen. Time to go to India. He wasn't hungry anyway. He studied the Burhi River C.P.R. on the top of the pile.

First off, he looked for the aberration. The computer's telltale note attached to the remake indicated flooding. Right. The river had overflowed its banks in a sparsely settled area. He checked for military installations on the overlay guide. He made some noncommittal notes on the report sheet, put it in a tube and let a pneumatic chute take it away. He didn't know where it went.

Than he looked at the whole photo-map. It looked like no other. By virtue of the acuity of the Sanroc C.P.R., Talon could pick up, under powerful magnification, a half-acre site and human forms visually. For higher visual magnification, Talon could delineate the area and request special processing. With that, he could spot a pack of cigarettes. The colors were strange, each indicating factual information, each a fingerprint of global reality. Different crops, individual types of plants could be identified; the progress in felling ancient timber stands, sugar-cane harvesting, disposition of troops and armor—all were identifiable. Earthquake, plant disease, fire and flood damage could be evaluated.

A tiny dot could be a funeral pyre in Benares. A family might be standing around a few burning logs on a ghat along the holy Ganges, beating the body to encourage the flames. A blue spread under a dry gully could be fresh water. In any event, the information would be noted, and that would be the end of it.

Talon liked the new area. He thought of Maharishi in the mountains. He rolled his mouth around the city names of Hyderabad and Lucknow and Janishedpur Balangir. The Sepoy Rebellion, the Kali-worshipping Thugs, and the Black Hole invaded his mind. *Four Feathers* and *Drums*, Alexander Korda's masterpieces of Fuzzy-Wuzzying, flashed through his head. Kipling. Christ, he hated looking and not touching. He was a voyeur into the world of others, down to a cigarette pack. But he wanted to be there.

He saw under his powerful magnifying lens a white spot in Nepal, just across the border, near the Indian city of Jalesmar. He magnified further and saw, at that northeast edge of his forty by forty-inch working photo of the ten-mile-square area an impression of catastrophe. At 500x magnification, he could make out furious flames. A burning granary and farm, he thought.

The pain of man. He fixed the coordinates and ordered up a 15x computer magnification of the area from an adjacent section, which would show the burning area better because of edge overlap. Next week he could see the before and after of personal human disaster. Voyeurism.

Before he left at five-thirty, he finished four more section reports and ordered up highly magnified coordinates for the nude beach at San Gregorio in California.

He wondered whether she'd show up.

5

"Charley?"

"Yes."

"This is Miss Dawson."

"Hi, Peg."

"Charley, I think there's a problem." From her desk the prim and fiftyish Margaret Dawson looked out over her console at a large number of other clerical types who nurtured the Company's central computer.

"Well, Peg, let's see if we can solve it. What seems to be the matter?"

"A request for a C.P.R. came in for one of our proprietary areas."

On the other end of the line a pair of shoes hit the floor and Charley's calm voice belied a high discomfort level. "You're sure?"

"Quite sure. I double-checked the time-base recorder, and—well, it was called in. What shall I do?"

"No problem, Peg, no problem. It's likely a simple error by the reader. A miscue? Anyway, I can't possibly imagine any sort of exposure. After all, we have covered the bases, haven't we?"

"Yes." She hesitated a moment, then said, "What shall I do about the request?"

Charley thought a moment. "We can't very well hold it up, can we? It won't show anything. Send it right along, and we'll take the necessary steps to check it out. Now, don't you concern yourself for a moment. All right, Peg?"

"If you say so."

"Of course I do. Now which proprietary area was it?"

"R201."

"Yes, yes. That's Talon. He's been reading that section for about a month. Well, we'll take care of the problem. All better?"

"Yes, I think so."

"Good work. You know, I think there'll be a little bonus for you this month."

"Thank you."

"Now, don't worry; everything is fine."

"All right."

"Goodbye, Peg."

"Goodbye, Charley."

Charley hung up and pulled at his pants. It was a habit that he had acquired twenty years before permanent press and double-knits. His suit was new, but it still looked wrinkled. Sensitive operations made him sweat constantly. He looked worried.

6

Talon got off the subway at six-fifteen, shopped at a bodega on Amsterdam Avenue, and walked into his apartment at quarter to seven. She couldn't be as fine as he thought.

He thought of the foxes at Huntington Beach and Newport, and put on "California Dreamin'." He was mashing up pinto beans, jalapeño peppers, Tabasco and black olives for bean dip, when the downstairs doorbell rang.

He picked up an ancient earphone and yelled into the metal grill in the kitchen wall.

"Hello?"

"Joe, it's me, Carlee. It's seven."

"Right, it's seven." A little after. He'd been watching seconds.

"Well, how do I get in?" Her voice was metallic over the earphone.

"Just open the door and come up to the first floor." He pushed a button on the grill, and he could hear the electric latch buzzing through the earphone. He remembered the surfboard and that he'd forgotten to call Ghost and the super.

He heard a lot of thumping coming up the stairs. He abandoned the idea of jettisoning the ten-foot board out his window. What's face, anyway? He went to the door to let her in.

She was wearing faded Levis and a matching jacket with a shearling wool collar. She had on a pair of Vibram-soled Eddie Bauer hiking boots that looked like they'd been around. She had on a kelly-green turtleneck sweater. She was dragging an enormous suitcase. He wanted to hold his breath.

"I'll help you."

"No, thanks." She looked determined as she pulled the suitcase through the door.

"It's bigger than you are."

"I'm moving."

"Oh?"

"I was staying at the Rehearsal Club—it's a women's residence near Twenty-One." She got it out between breaths.

"You're puffing."

"So're you."

"I just ran up from the store." He gestured to the cutting board on the sink, where the bean dip lay in a gray mass.

"Liar," she said, stripping off her jacket.

He took the coat and noted the contents of the sweater. Not

only was he short of breath, he was shaking a bit. He hung her jacket in the broom closet. "How was the . . ."

"Visitors' Bureau?"

"Yeah," he said, leading her into the living room.

She spotted the ancient surfboard right off. "Early sixties, eh?"

"Um," he said. "Want a drink?" Presto chango.

"Sure. Got scotch and water?"

"Done."

"Tall."

"Right," he said. She was reclining on the sofa. He'd never featured spending much on furniture. It was a bit ratty.

He went into the kitchen to get the drinks and dip. He heard her yelling over the Mamas and the Papas: "It looks like you got this stuff from some fraternity house."

He wanted to put the mummy's curse on the two Princeton-type thieves who had sold him most of the junk. Them and their Old Nassau and their orange-and-black hearts.

"But I really like it," he heard over his shoulder. She was standing in the kitchen. "Most of the creeps in this town have all this stuff in glass and chrome and seduction shades of Peter Max. I haven't seen a scooter tire loose in a living room in days. And the antediluvian surfing device is camp, not kitsch."

"Huh?"

"*Not* grotesquely and expensively plastic."

"Oh, yeah—kitsch." He had the drinks, bean dip and Health Valley pure corn chips assembled on the cutting board. He trotted it all into the living room. They both sat. He handed her the scotch and hit on his vodka and tonic with lots of real, squeezed lime.

"What's for dinner?" she said.

"In a hurry?"

"No, I'm just not awfully hungry."

"Me either."

"I'm not going to do it right off, you know. I've never been that way. I've got too many things I want to do and places to see to get involved. And I won't do it without real involvement. There's not enough to it."

"Right. I'm the same way."

"Liar."

"I'm not Don Jose from Far Rockaway."

"Where?"

"Nowhere. I mean, it's some place in Brooklyn or somewhere."

"Anyway, I want to be sure you know where we stand."

"Right."

"Liar."

"No, it's a deal. No rush, no muss, no fuss." He put on the Beach Boys—"California Girls." He knew she meant what she said. He also knew something else. "You can sleep on the couch. There are some extra drawers there"—he pointed at the thousand-dollar rosewood Cadovious wall system which housed his stereo. "And I'll clear some space in the bathroom."

She started crying again. He heard her burble, "How did you know?"

"Psychic," he said, assuming the position, her head on his chest. He really was in no rush, but, Christ, she cried a lot. "I mean, it's all the time that chicks poke me with umbrellas in the morning, tell me they're not hot for my body, and move in at night. Sometimes twice a week. This is the Big Apple."

She was running down. "They gave me a ticket back to Honolulu."

He got a sinking sensation.

"I cashed it in." She reached in her pocket and pulled out some bills. She pressed a twenty into his hand.

He felt much better and tried to give it back.

"No, it's only temporary. Everything split even, okay?"

"Sure, it's a deal."

"I'm going to look for a job tomorrow." She brightened up. "Got a *Times*?"

"Just Wednesday's."

"Do the crossword yet?"

"No, I was saving it in case I was too hungover to really get after the Sunday model."

While they were scribbling on the crossword, he got a chance to ogle her. She had the whole thing. High cheekbones, wide mouth with real lips, freckles, an important but unobtrusive nose. A slight overbite. Good chin. Great skin. Color without blush-on. He barely suppressed a moan.

He made more drinks, and they talked. He was reasonably amusing. She was receptive. She laughed a lot.

They took a walk to Central Park West, and they looked at the cast-iron dragons on the fence around the San Remo. It was cold out, and her hand, as he held it, was warm and cool at the same time. They walked west on Seventy-sixth and explored Amsterdam Avenue. She'd never known these places existed. The walk became a hike as they went by the darkened Museum of Natural History and entered the forbidden evening environs of Central Park. They walked out of the park, and he pointed out the venerable Dakota, the medieval-looking co-op where Rosemary had her devilish baby.

They walked to Lincoln Center, and he told her about watching Leontyne Price do the modern Cleopatra. In three hours of walking, he told her all about himself, his scooter, his surfing. Everything except his job and his ambitions.

It wasn't that he told her everything to impress her; it was just that he had this overpowering urge to communicate. She was perceptive, beautiful, graceful and cool. And warm.

She was amazed at all the things he'd read. One whole

wall of his living room was books. She couldn't believe he'd read them all. She said T. E. Lawrence was like that— supposedly he'd read all the books at Cambridge or Oxford. He held back from telling her that he'd read everything ever printed about Lawrence, but did say that he rather fancied himself to be like Lawrence, except for the sexual details. The rule and exception showed him to be a master of understatement.

Sometimes they held hands; sometimes they didn't. When they didn't, it was okay, because he knew she'd soon reach for his again. Or vice versa.

Sometimes, when she was excited about something, she pranced on those long legs. Sometimes she gave him a small peck on the cheek.

He still poked her every once in a while. She knew why.

The walk was over too soon. He got that special feeling that all their times together would be over too soon. It knocked him out. He looked at things through her eyes.

They walked into the apartment, and she pulled the suitcase into the living room. She started to take out long things.

"Where can I hang these?"

"I use a chifforobe in the bedroom. I've got the closet set up for photo work and tools." And other things, he thought. "I'll clear the stuff out of the broom closet for you." He didn't want to talk. He was afraid he'd say something wrong and she'd disappear. Run out the door screaming at him.

He got the closet ready, put the tire in his room, and cleared the medicine cabinet. He took an extra pillow and his sleeping bag from a drawer and carried them into the living room. He got out a pillowcase, towel and face cloth and put them on the couch. She was still rooting around in her stuff.

He noticed a smell like babies in the apartment. It was baby powder. Its smell was all around her. He went back into the bedroom, turned on the light and started reading a J. P. Donleavy novel.

He thought about the fire he'd seen in the satellite photo. He felt strangely omnipotent with his spy-in-the-sky world view. He thought about ordering up a C.P.R. to check the surf at the Pipeline on Oahu.

He saw a red-flannel figure go by the open bedroom door. It couldn't be true. A few minutes later, he heard the sound of bottles on the bathroom shelf and then the shower going.

He stripped and turned off the light, opened the casement window and got into bed. Later he felt a kiss and touched a flannel arm, and she was gone. He put on a robe, took a shower, removed his contacts and went back to bed. Thank you, God, he thought.

7

Saturday morning Talon awoke feeling peculiar. It was the result of no hangover, reduced morning mouth, and the sleeping blond-topped red-flannel lump poised on the edge of his bed. He pulled himself into a sitting position and fumbled with his watch. Nine-twelve. He relaxed, closed his eyes, and started his meditation. Thoughts came to him as he repeated the mantra, principally the urge to poke the flannel for confirmation.

Eight minutes into the meditation, the flannel poked him.

"What are you doing?" the lovely voice asked.

"Meditating."

"Didn't your mother tell you that was nasty?"

"I'll be through in a while." He opened an eye and checked his watch. "Twelve minutes, okay?"

"Okay."

He heard some rustling, and the bed jiggled. Damn, he said to himself. The Maharishi is impinging on my love life. He got the mantra going again, but he was aware of noises in the kitchen. He neglected the two minutes of time necessary to wind down from the meditation. It made him a little edgy, but he wanted to bite the red flannel.

"When did you invade the sacred sanctum?"

"About five A.M.; I got cold."

"That's a down bag."

"It was too hot with the nightshirt."

"Oh."

"I was very careful not to disturb you." She looked much smaller and very fragile in the red tent. She was beautiful.

"I know." He helped her locate a frying pan, and she started to break eggs.

"Your eyes were brown yesterday."

"Brown contacts. I get tired of looking at the same face in the morning. I tried a moustache, but my employer frowned on it."

"Interesting morning conversation, too."

"Right."

"When does the maid come?" She pointed at the mass of kitchenware piled in the sink.

"I don't have one."

"You still don't. Why don't we split it up? I cook; you clean. If you cook, I clean."

"Okay."

"Otherwise, you'll have to start using the bathtub for all that."

"Fine."

"I'm not really bossy. I just think we'd better get the signals straight."

She came over to him then and wrapped her arms around his neck. He could feel her through his robe and her flannels. He held her close, and she held him. She put her cheek against his. His head pounded. Then she let go. He did, too. Reluctantly.

"I'm glad you didn't kiss me," he said.

"Why?"

"That almost gave me a coronary."

She colored. "Me too."

"That was fine."

"I figured you needed some reassurance. It was those staccato answers."

"Me? Never."

"Liar."

They got back to making breakfast. He figured she was too good to be human. "You an android?"

"Huh?" She had gracefully gotten some egg white on her flannel.

"Android."

"I heard it the first time. What's an android?" She finished cleaning it off.

"A machine. Programmed to do things. A robot. The perfect plastic person. . . . Sci-fi." Something had gone wrong. She looked very upset. It took him ten minutes of bright talk to get her back on the track.

"If I had a waffle iron, I'd make you waffles," she said finally, with a few sniffs.

"If I had a Lear Jet, we'd be eating them on the way to visit my bowling alley in Newport Beach."

"You have a bowling alley in California?"

"No, but if I had the bread for the Lear, the bowling alley would be peanuts."

That broke it, and not one more sour note played through breakfast, the walk through Central Park and the visit to the Museum of Art and the zoo. By the time they got to the dormant fountain at Fifty-ninth Street and Fifth Avenue, it was after two and they were bushed.

"The Plaza Hotel for drinks or Rumpelmayer's for ice cream?"

"Wine, wine," she said, galloping around on her giraffe legs.

"Done," he said, heading her toward the Plaza and civilization.

"I think I'm falling in love with you," she said.

"Oh," he said.

"So if I say something after the wine, you know I thought about it first."

"Right." His head was pounding again.

"You like me, too, huh?"

Talon, he said to himself, this time it's got to be right. One wrong word and she'll evaporate. Just one. "Right, Jane," he said, and started scratching under his arms and jumping around with bent knees. "I like screw." He waited for the world to collapse while he continued to play Cheetah.

People were looking. It was time-lapse photography. He watched her eye corners wrinkle up with dismay. He started thinking about apologies. It was too late.

Then the tide came in. She started laughing.

"You rotten Talon!" she screamed at him. He'd heard worse. "You cool bastard!" She chased him all the way to Trader Vic's.

8

"Great place."

"I spend a lot of time and money here."

"Oh," she said.

"No one special."

She looked relieved.

"Why monkey around with my affections?" she asked.

He guffawed appreciatively. "It all started when I was asked to serve as the alternate judge for the Miss Newport Beach contest. The local Jaycees were putting on the show."

"Huh?"

"A meat market. More foxes than Harrow ever had."

"Huh?"

"Anyway, I had this fantasy."

"Oh." She started to perk up.

"I saw myself in this Mack Sennett gorilla suit, right? With the obsidian chest and low brow. I mean, the whole trip."

"Uh huh."

"So, I run up on the stage like King Kong. . . ."

"Queen Kong." She giggled.

"I'm telling the story. Okay? So I run up on the stage and grab one of the young lovelies and throw her over my shoulder. . . ."

"One of the small ones."

"Right. And I'm running out the emergency exit with this fluff over my back and everyone screaming . . ."

"Especially her parents, who have each brought their new spouses to see her win."

"Right, so I'm running out, and this little lady twists and says in my ear, 'Hey, far out! I never did it with a gorilla before.'"

She cracked up. Then she looked serious. "Suppose . . ."

"Suppose what?" He was happy with his story.

"Suppose she'd turned and said, 'Hey, man, cut it out! I'm tired of doing it with gorillas.' "

I'm in love, he thought.

"Or 'Quit monkeying around with me.'"

"All right," he said. "Enough. No more gorilla stories, okay?"

"Okay." She put her hand on his leg.

He knew he never wanted to stand up again, anyway.

An hour later, he'd been through three glasses of red and the best sit-down brass-rail elbow-bending bar talk that had ever been his pleasure. It flowed like the Big Mo. Solid and satisfying. And he still couldn't stand up.

"What happened this morning?" he asked.

"The . . ."

"Android?"

"Yes, the android thing?"

"Right."

"That's serious," she said.

"Right, now we're serious. I'm sorry."

"I thought you were looking through me. I got scared."

"Is there something to see?" He wanted to kick himself.

"Do you want to look?"

Answer a question with a question. Damn. What could he say? Especially when he couldn't stand up. "No."

They were quiet for a while. He was miserable.

"Let's go home," she said.

It was the way she said "home." He didn't say anything. He paid, and they got into a cab.

When they walked into the apartment, she headed for the

bedroom. When he got there, she was lying on her stomach on the bed. She was shaking.

"Sorry about the boots." Her voice came muffled by the pillow.

"Right," he said as he took off his shoes. He pulled off her boots.

"I only met you yesterday."

"Right."

"It wasn't the wine," she said as he snuggled up next to her.

"We can wait until tonight."

"Liar."

9

It had been a very slow process, unwrapping that package. Not planned; it just happened that way. It was late in the afternoon, and the light that came in through the floor-to-ceiling casement windows showed her nestled against him, head on his shoulder, lips touching his neck.

He remembered things in his mind's eye. Soft marshmallows on a woman's firm breasts. Soft, downy hair between her legs. She smelled of baby powder all over. Soft skin, cool and smooth. Long thin legs, opening to him. Lips. Arms. He fell asleep.

He woke up again at nine o'clock. He'd missed his evening meditation. He realized she was still asleep on his shoulder, but his arm was not numb. What a woman.

She stirred. "That was marvelous."

"Thanks. Do you ever wake up grouchy?"

"Never."

"Do you ever get grouchy?"

"Rarely."

They started touching each other. Afterward, she slept again.

The lovemaking itself had been dynamite. He felt as though he had taken Samarkand and left the skulls of a hundred thousand of the enemy piled high at the gate. He was Tamerlane asserting his right to select the most beautiful woman in the land. And here she was.

He sat up in bed and started his meditation, but the intensity of the feelings, her smoothness and movements—economical but sensual—kept crowding out the mantra. It all tumbled down on him.

He kept after the meditation. He had no doubts that it gave him more energy, made him more calm, more alert. He was committed to it.

Then suddenly he knew that his twenty minutes were up. They had disappeared. He winked one eye open and checked his watch. Then slowly he opened his eyes.

It was dark in the room. He reached under the sheet and felt her. Everything she did, every move she made was right. Cool and warm and hot, all at once. Pure and simple. She brought something else to lovemaking: a quiet f.

He never thought much. He reacted, intuited. The answers came to him from the depths. Words flowed, movements came, decisions were made, and the years went by without intent. Like riding a wave. And she was a wave. The symbiosis and separation of the first and last great nonsport, the man on the wave.

First the wait. The wait for the perfect wave. You seek it in California, Australia, Hawaii. Maybe this one—no, too fast. That one? Damn—missed it, the wall slipping past. On and on. Dawn to dusk. Moondogging on a bright Malibu night. Close, but never there.

Except in the mind. There, it forms up. The combination of Huntington Pier, Waimea Bay, Cannons, the Ranch, Point Panic, Dunes, Sunset, the Bonsai Pipeline. Five feet and twenty-five feet at the same time. Quick-forming and slow-rolling. Huge drop and fast right and left. A head-dipping, toe-hanging, hundred-yard tunnel with a shoulder.

And when it's over, when the tunnel's run and the perfect one has rolled by and all the adrenaline has pumped, you want it again. You look to see who saw, and you feel that there may yet be one more. Somewhere. So you work your way outside again and wait.

There she was, breathing next to him. A woman for all seasons. He walked a beach of shingle with her. Any other way but workaday. He needed a Hellespont, a Goliath, a Cyclops. He had conquered the unconquerable. But only for the moment. All he knew couldn't help him. He pulled her to him and held her tightly.

The mind involvement was the thing. It inspired festering attacks of libido in him that took them well into Sunday morning. At eleven they showered, he shaved, and she shooed him out the door to get the *Times*. He returned to a whirlwind of activity. He noticed and failed to comment on the fact that the sleeping bag had disappeared from the living room. He surreptitiously checked and found it back in the drawer. She had made up his bed with both pillows. He felt great.

"Mornin', pal," he said.

"Good morning, you beautiful man."

"You have a glow about you this day. A veritable aurora."

"It's the diet."

"I haven't eaten anything since a week ago. You like Eggs Benedict?"

She looked impressed. "Sure. You make-a da Hollandaise?"

"Why-a shoo, bambino mio. Eet's a-simple. You take one

cab, add you and me, gently stir and heat in the back seat on the way to the Algonquin Hotel, and presto!"

"Voilà!"

"Whatever."

"I'm ready."

"We go." He tucked the *Times* under his arm.

10

"I don't know anything about you," she announced halfway through the Sunday puzzle. "All you do is talk and use those winsome, wicked ways and never say anything." She pouted.

He drank some coffee and looked around the Algonquin's dining room. "This is where they all came, you know. All the writers. Newsmen. Critics. They sat and talked. Maybe they still do."

"Huh?"

"Alton Cook, Benchley, Al Eisenstaedt, Dr. David Pearce, Fred Allen, Agee, people like that. This was the place to stay and chat and eat supper."

"It's nice. Old and funky. I wonder how the massage-parlor set affects business?"

"This is an oasis. Jane, it's a jungle out there."

"Thank you, Lord Greystroke."

"Stoke."

"I know what you do, Tarzan."

"Got me."

"So answer. Will the real Joe Talon please stand up?"

"All in good time. Aside from surfing and crops, I'm like Switzerland. Neutral."

"Cold?"

"Only when you weren't in my territory."

"Is it yours?"

"Ours if you like."

"Yes."

"All right. Ours." He got a combination of sick and happy in the feeling department. At gut level, before he threw her across his pommel and rode off on a white horse to Camelot, he wanted to spill it. The works. The frustrations, the plans, the dreams. The schizoid thing was eating him at the "ours" level. There was no "ours" at the Company. Only first person singular. He was the spy who never was.

"Do you work tomorrow?"

He came back from his pretended perusal of the crossword. "Right."

"I'll start looking for work on Tuesday, then. Tomorrow I'll clean up and get organized."

"Terrific."

"You don't sound very enthusiastic."

"I don't know, Carlee."

"It wasn't the wine. I told you."

"Right." Was that only yesterday? Why did she always have to say the perfect thing? He got a feeling of good in his belly. "It's just that it's going like a runaway freight train."

"I'm supposed to say that. Are you afraid I'll run away?"

"Fifty-fifty between your running away and being there."

"Oh." She looked hurt.

He couldn't say anything. He wanted to bring them down. But he didn't want to blow it. Not yet.

"Say something, Tarzan."

"You pain."

She giggled that giggle. They got back on the track and continued to highball.

He walked behind her Levis on the way out. He felt a growl coming. Why did beauty, grace, fine lines, and an ass so tight it squeaked do such things to him? He wanted to take some time off, grab a flight to Acapulco with Carlee, and hump and laugh until he was sick and tired of her. Say, ten years.

He sure didn't get tired of her that afternoon. Or that evening. Or Monday morning. He even thought about revising his time horizons in the subway, on the way to work.

11

"Morning, Moneypenny."

"Morning, Funnypecker."

"Truce?"

"Truce." She'd finally broken it. Talon noticed that she was thrusting herself at him with a monumentally straight back. The resultant effect on her chest was staggering. Newton's Third Law. "At ease. Your thrill of victory is affecting my privates."

"And cut that stuff out, too," she said. "You are the only boor in this department."

"What department is that?"

She made like she never asked herself that question. Words from the past came. "None of your business," she said.

"Up your business, too," he mumbled.

"What?"

He was almost at the door where his second life began. "Nothing. Truce." He went in.

Because of the way the department was laid out physically, Talon seldom saw any of his workmates. Some, he figured, he never saw. And he wouldn't know what they did or who they were if he did run into them.

He waited a full five minutes after stepping into his analysis carrel before dialing his home number. The line was busy. He felt neutral. She was still there, but who was she calling? He dialed again, and the phone rang.

"Hello?" She definitely had the most beautiful voice in the whole world.

"Hi, it's Talon."

"Hi, Joe. I'm still here."

"Right."

"I called Ghost. They'll come to pick up your bike at noon. The guy said things are slow, and it can be finished soon. So maybe we can pack into the wilderness this weekend. It'll be cold, and we can snuggle. What do you think?"

Making plans for a week ahead. His stomach churned. "Huh? Well, that sounds okay. Tell him to put a sissy bar on and to straighten the left foot peg and . . ."

"Wait, I've got to get a pencil."

Witch. Moving into his life. It was too wonderful to last. He hated it.

"Okay. Sissy bar, left peg and . . .?"

"Get it running. Plugs, oil change, tune it good. Check the lights. Dunlop rear tire."

"You're getting a new one?"

"Right."

"Can I throw out the one in the living room?"

"I was going to have the Jolly Green Giant in for quoits."

Flat. Domesticity was going to kill it.

"Ho, ho. A pox on you, my goodly host."

She liked it? Damn. He had to do something wrong. If he didn't, he'd never know. "Right. Send the tire airmail."

"I don't get it."

"That's garbage in Harlem. They airmail it. Out the windows."

"Ho, ho."

"Well, so long."

"Wait. I don't know where your bike is. I've got to call Ghost back."

"It's at the Liss Garage. Seventy-first between Ninth and Tenth avenues."

"Okay, boss. Get ready for some truckin'."

"Right."

"I love you."

"It's the wine."

"Hic."

"Like a hangover."

"I bet you say that to all the girls."

"Right."

"Goodbye, hardnose."

" 'Bye, and thanks."

"Any time."

He hung up. And felt stupid. The most beautiful woman in the whole world had practically plighted her troth to him. And she didn't seem like your run-of-the-mill plighter. Hello Mr. Cool, goodbye Carlee.

12

He picked up a cardboard tube of C.P.R. prints from the N.R.O. computer and pulled them out. He spent the morning checking the enlargements against his Friday notes on aberrations. Lunch, as usual, he ordered out.

Lunch hour was for eating Italian-sausage and meatball heros, checking surf and bodies on his personal request prints, and daydreaming about being a spy instead of a reconnaissance reader.

He leafed through the new C.P.R.s. He picked out the latest Ranch print he'd ordered. Two miles from California's Point Concepcion and one of surfing's legends, he'd skimmed the even, right-breaking four-foot waves when he was fifteen. The ocean. The only thing that doesn't change, but that's never the same, he said to himself as he looked at the lines of waves coming in on the print.

Carlee kept coming into his mind. She had a mile-wide mouth. The corners turned up and made very tiny noises when she smiled. Which was often.

He was thinking about her when he almost missed the Sanroc print that didn't make any sense at all.

The lap-over print of his pinpoint farm disaster had the right coordinates, time, date, section references and phase. It was a picture of the hundred-square-mile area just north of the portion of India and part of Nepal that he'd looked at the previous Friday. But every bit of it was covered with storm clouds.

It seemed unlikely to him that the clouds would be perfectly square along the section lines. The C.P.R. had to overlap the burning farm. But it showed only clouds. It made no sense. He butted the Q201 print from Friday up against what was supposed the be the R201 print. No question. On the same day, with the same scan, no more than one and a half minutes apart, one print was clear as a bell and the other was obscured by heavy clouds. What showed was not possible.

He wrote up an order for C.P.R.s R200 and R202, the adjacent quadrant numbers. He wrote up an order for infrared prints of the R201 area. Then he spent the rest of his lunch hour checking the surf at the Ranch and the nudes at Venice Beach, and thereby he dismissed the storm clouds.

Miss D'Arcy let him know at three-thirty that Flynn wanted to see him.

"Afternoon, Joe," Flynn said.

"Right."

"You know, Joe, I've been in this business a long time. . . ."

History again. Talon started to turn off. If he had been a cat, the film would have been sliding across his eyes. He adjusted himself in the chair. He slowed his breathing. And he prepared to slip into pause-filling affirmatives. "Right."

"And, as an administrator, I know that leeway for you folks is critical; especially you, Joe. Your production is better than any two of the other people working the Sanroc."

Talon perked up. That was the first indication he'd ever had of his value. Not to mention that he'd never even been told anyone else was doing what he did. That's the way things were. Life with the Company was a series of conjectures, a schizoid world of eternal paranoids. But here he sensed something else. Somehow a crack was opening. The film slid back. "Right." He nodded his head as if he'd known all along.

"So there haven't been many questions about your print requests."

"Humoring me."

Flynn ignored him. "Now, Joe, each of those prints costs the Company nine hundred and sixty-seven dollars."

Good. "So?"

"So what are you doing with San Gregorio, Venice, Point Reyes and Seal Beach? Not to mention Minorca and Corsica . . ."

Talon stared at the wizened face behind the desk. Flynn was steepling his fingers. Dale Carnegie would have been proud of him. Honesty shone through his eyes, and if his horn-rimmed glasses had been freznelled, Talon would have been blinded instead of merely transfixed. "Right."

"That's not an answer, Joe. I have to have an answer. In the last year alone, you've requested more than two hundred coordinates outside your area. I need an answer. That's nearly two hundred thousand dollars' worth, Joe."

"Call it a perquisite."

"Judas Priest! Joe, I need an explanation. I stand up for you, but this is too much!"

Very waspy, that "Judas Priest" stuff, Talon thought. Eastern waspy. "I want a real job."

Exasperation pulled at the corners of Flynn's eyes. "Please, Joe. Not now. The orders are clear. With every request from now on, you'll need an aberration report."

"Tits and surf." What the hell. If you can't tell your mother, who can you tell?

"I beg your pardon?"

"I check the nude beaches and my favorite old surfing areas. Nostalgia. Escape. Innocence. It keeps me out of trouble at lunchtime."

"They'll never buy it."

"In the words of my sainted Jewish grandmother, I should care."

"Joe."

"M."

"Joe, cut it out."

"Look, I try to square it with you, and you don't believe me. I quit."

"Impossible. Anyway, for what it's worth, I do believe you."

"Vot den?"

"I beg your pardon, Joe?"

"Translated, it means 'So?'"

"I'll make a memo."

"The aberration reports?"

"Until we get this straightened out." Flynn started shuffling papers.

Talon walked out humming "The Times They Are a-Changin'."

13

Back in his carrel, Talon tried to figure out who was responsible for the crinkle in his guts: Flynn, Carlee, or Sanroc. He gained confidence in the answer when the refusal of his last requests came burping out of the pneumatic tube beside his desk. His heart wasn't in his work the rest of the day, but what the hell? he thought, there's always tomorrow.

On the way out that afternoon he walked through some adjacent offices of the Department of Agriculture. He figured they weren't Company-related, since some of the people were black, and from time to time he saw them actually enjoying the comfort of human intercourse over coffee in true bureaucratic style. Now it was five-thirty, and there was not a soul around.

He scouted for things he felt could enhance his fantasies. It was in his blood.

From time to time he picked up franked envelopes which he used for personal purposes, despite their plain warnings of castration or worse. He lifted official stationery, thinking he might use it sometime. At one time he had seriously considered sending Flynn an eviction notice, but backed off, sure in the knowledge that the blame would be immediately and unerringly pegged in the correct location.

He had adopted the principle of acquiring or carrying away articles of potential value to an operative some years before. His closet at home contained a lot more than Ag stationery. It was the focus of his fantasies. Among other things, he had corporate seals, etching and engraving equipment, photo-enlarging and reducing gear, a check protector, bank stationery from Chase, Chemical, and Irving Trust, a check encoder, blank checks, stock certificates, lock-picking and key duplication equipment, and a black box.

He had tools. He had a gun—an Armalite .22 semi-automatic rifle, which folded up in its plastic stock. With his tools he had fashioned a reasonably adequate silencer for the weapon. That was easy. He just ordered prints of the patents he'd looked up in the Forty-second Street branch of the New York Public Library.

He had all kinds of stuff there. Walter Mitty's answer to Fibber McGee's closet.

For some weeks he had been eyeing a portable teletype machine, the kind used for computer terminals. Just put a phone handset into the cradle and dial. Assuming that you knew the computer's phone number and the code to get access to the program or memory bank, it was a piece of cake. It could come in handy.

Talon knew numbers. He dialed them every day.

This particular machine, a little larger than a portable typewriter, was sitting on some Aggie's desk, the cover leaning casually against the wall. Talon coiled the power cord and put it on top of the keys. He removed the accordion-pleated computer paper from the roller and put a stack of it on top of the power cord. He put the cover on. He hefted the machine and carried it into the men's room.

He locked a toilet door, left the computer terminal and climbed out over the partition. He walked back to his office, telling Miss D'Arcy on the way that he'd forgotten his purse. In his office, Talon picked up a small bottle of black model dope which he used for marking photos.

Back in the men's room, he carefully painted out "Property U.S. Government." He waved at the guard when he left the building.

Talon was surprised at his lack of adrenaline as he pushed through the subway turnstile. He got a seat on the train and thought that maybe living out his fantasies wasn't the answer. But then again, he didn't know what the answer was.

14

He realized that he'd forgotten his morning meditation as he lugged his prize home. It was East Coast dark, New York dark outside, and the Museum glowered at him momentarily as he crossed Seventy-seventh Street and walked along Central Park West. His gut was cringing as he turned west on Seventy-fifth. He knew she wouldn't be there.

But she was.

"Hi."

"Mph." Her mouth cut off his word of greeting. Her arms were around his neck. He thought about getting an EKG.

"I've been home all day."

The portion of the apartment that he could see looked as though a thousand elves with toothbrushes had been scrubbing for a year. "Right," he said.

He wanted to ask her to twitch her nose again and make everything the way it was before. Instead he let her lead him by the hand, seat him on the couch, and remove his shoes. She switched off the Beach Boys, who were doing their thing, and stepped into the kitchen.

"I've got some odds and ends to finish up while you meditate, Joe. Dinner at eight."

He couldn't believe it. He pushed his newly acquired teletype into the right position for a footrest and started the mantra.

Twenty minutes later he stopped the mantra. He felt refreshed. He got his contacts unstuck, and he looked around. There on the table next to him was a large glass containing ice and a clear liquid. Submerged was an olive, pimento removed. His eyes watered. He reached for the glass.

He stretched out on the couch and thought about his last talk with Flynn. Between Flynn and Carlee, he felt very depressed. It was the years of control, of trying to be on top of situations. They added up. Now, in a few days, his world was collapsing and inflating at the same time.

He felt those lips light on his.

"It's eight."

"Right."

"Soup's on."

"Right."

"Open your eyes!"

"Right." He got up and followed her into the kitchen. Sitting at the tiny dining table left him no alternative but to look into her eyes. He played with the vichyssoise, which she had to have made from scratch, trying to sink the parsley.

She must have memorized *Larousse gastronomique*. Through the haze, he tasted enough to realize that she knew what she was doing. She didn't feed him too much; she herself hardly ate at all. He grunted appreciatively from time to time. Mostly they looked at each other. She really had the eyes for looking. He wanted to be playing in the waves with her, somewhere.

After dinner they sipped some wine. She turned on the radio and found a rock station. She did the Bump for twenty minutes around the living room, swirling in her pink outfit, never missing a beat. He watched in awe. She sat, out of breath, at his feet while he tried to figure out what was wrong.

He knew—had known all along. It was the Company. He had to share everything with her. Or nothing. There was no way out of it. It wasn't only the moles who had hidden lives. No one in the Company told anyone anything. He had to work it out soon. Or else she'd be gone.

15

Talon was in a daze Tuesday. It was nearly noon when he realized that he'd forgotten his morning communion with the Maharishi and that none of his orders for prints had been filled—neither the California coast nor the lap-overs for R201, the storm cloud. It was depressing.

He dialed Octopus, the Company's central computer at Langley. He cradled the phone on his teletype and typed the access code through to the N.R.O.'s computer center in Washington. He added his personal code number and waited for an acknowledgment.

Octopus acknowledged his call with a double space on his terminal and the word "Go." He put in a formal request for the lap-overs and waited. The answer came back:

```
UNAUTHORIZED ACCESS-SPECIAL
REQUIREMENT ABERRATION MEMO FOR ALL
UNREPORTED ABERRANT PRINT ORDERS. BYE.
```

The connection died.

Frustration. He thought about making an aberration report on R201. He nearly wrote it up, but then he sat back and thought, Something is very strange. First the storm-cloud print, then a holdup on his personal requests. It is probably a shot into a very dark spot. But what the hell? Two birds with one stone. This was the boredom eliminator for his general lethargy and a new noontime kick. Take away my surf, huh? The bureaucratic bastards will rue the day. Maybe.

It was nearly lunchtime, so he called out for an Italian-sausage hero, and then he did a strange thing. He started cleaning up his carrel. In the seven years that he'd inhabited the cubicle, he'd never cleaned up. Months ago, high-security janitors had given up finding a place to dust. Now Talon gathered and sorted charts and photos, Kool butts, mummified pieces of hero sandwich, bits of donuts, scraps of paper with phone numbers. He was just scratching the surface. He dialed out to Miss D'Arcy for a broom.

He straightened out his diploma from U.C.L.A. He lined up his two pictures, one of Fred Hemmings dropping down a twenty-footer at Makaha, the other of Talon, bronzed and happy on the deck of the boat he had lived on for two years at Santa Cruz: the only bits of reality in the sci-fi environment he inhabited.

He kicked the orts into the hall. He sorted through the bits of paper he'd scrounged up and kept the few that had any meaning. All the research books, procedure books and code books, all the Company-issued information resources, which had been stacked in the corner or secreted under the desk, he set up on a shelf. Most of it he had locked up in his memory.

As he toiled, he entered the obliqueness of some long-due self-analysis. The cleanup worried him a bit. He wondered whether it eventuated from his new fantasy or from some latent nesting instinct triggered by Carlee. At any rate, by the end of the lunch hour he had decided that he was going from a slothful, reactive and intuitive life-style to one of heavy planning and introspection. He had gathered moss up to his eyeballs. No more.

He called Miss D'Arcy again and asked her to bring in the Panasonic pencil sharpener which he had long ago refused, having previously preferred his pocket knife. He also requested a Day-Timer for scheduling and a high-intensity lamp to ease his eye strain. He reminded her about the broom.

58

Miss D'Arcy's eyes bulged and her chest heaved, incidentally threatening the structural integrity of the building, when she personally delivered the supplies.

"What's happening?"

He wondered whether he was threatening the stability of her world. "I'm going straight."

"Seriously."

Looking at her opulence, he said, "It's plain as the nose on your face. If you can't beat 'em, join 'em."

She blushed nicely, the redness commencing at the exposed portions of her breasts and rising like the fluid in a thermometer to her hairline. "You haven't changed at all, you fink!"

"Ah, but I have. Dealings with the opposite sex take a bit longer as I sublimate my hitherto-unfettered libido." He leered at her deepening crimson cleavage.

"Beast." She scooted off down the hall.

As he finished up his ministrations, he found the bug. Not that it was unexpected. It didn't make much sense to him, since the phone was his only real communication with the world. It could have been tapped anywhere, and he had always supposed it was. He wondered whether he talked to himself. After five minutes of additional self-search, he thought perhaps he did. Cooped up in the carrel day after day. His sheer loneliness had been submerged in his sophomoric vicarious rambling on familiar beaches. And in talking to himself about it.

The bug was just another sign that he had to redirect his activities. His private world had been invaded. All else was theirs. Just the noon hour of his solitude had been his own. Now that too had been exposed. His resolve firmed up, and he vowed that this Caesar had really crossed the Rubicon. Covert, shmovert, he thought. I'm going to dig up this anthill.

In this, the fifth month of his thirty-seventh year, he

whispered to himself, Today I am a man. He spent a few minutes contemplating that; then he organized the pile of request C.P.R.s that he had ordered for his lunchtime reverie. He added R201 to the middle of the pile and put a note on top indicating that he was through with them.

His carrel had taken on the sterility it had had the first day he walked into it. And never since, until now.

He attacked the prints that represented the bulk of his week's work, furiously shuffling through them. By five-thirty he had completed them, completed his aberration reports and orders for close-ups. He hummed and whistled a lot to give whoever was listening to him something to keep busy with. He wanted to call Carlee, but felt the intrusion of the Company was too much to live with, now that it had been confirmed.

16

Charley dialed and then waited impatiently until the customary fourth ring sounded on the other end of the phone line.

"Hello?"

"Mr. Bowles, this is Charley."

"Yes, Charles?"

"It's about our Nepal proprietary."

"Yes?"

"The reader on that section ordered up a print."

"Error or what, Charles? After all, why would anyone order up a print of nothing?" He sounded impatient. As usual.

60

"Well, sir, I don't know. I wasn't going to bother with calling you at all, but some rather strange data have turned up on the man. I initiated some additional work."

"What about the normal surveillance?"

"Yes, sir. That is going along quite smoothly. But since we have never been confronted by this sort of situation, I thought . . ."

"Quite right, Charles. Go on."

"This reader was checked by a pro team last Friday, after he arrived late at the section."

"Oh?"

"The pro team gave him quite a thorough going-over."

"So?"

"Well, he lied on the polygraph."

"Come, Charles. You of all people know what these clerk types are like. Bottom rung. They all lie. Can't be helped."

"I know that, sir. But this time the polygraph did not pick it up. We know that he lied by virtue of our other data. He definitely fooled the machine."

"We both know that's possible. Well, what's the upshot of all this? Do you think he is a renegade?"

Charley hesitated. "Well, I don't know."

"When you do, please call back. In the meantime, Charles, keep close tabs on him. You know what to do if it is necessary."

"Yes, sir."

"Goodbye, Charles."

"Goodbye, Mr. Bowles." Charley pulled his pants up at the knees and stared out the window at Langley Forest.

17

The next three nights were important to Talon. He grew steadily closer to Carlee. During the three days he sat like Nero Wolfe in the tiny carrel, eyes closed, lips humming or singing, and rustling papers regularly. In his mind he was formulating a plan with which to attack the problem his mind had posited.

He had drawn fifteen hundred dollars from his savings account, to add to the cash reserve he kept hidden at home in the closet. Three hundred-odd dollars he gave to Carlee to pay Ghost for the scooter, which was to be delivered on Friday. He also gave her keys to his apartment. He was on the point of handing over his heart as well on Wednesday night, but he figured that would have to wait, pending his rationalization of his schizoid life.

He ate sparingly and dressed better. He regularly moved through his Aikido exercises and started to feel his long muscles tone up. He found time for his meditations and felt more alive than he had for longer than he cared to think about.

Carlee had looked at him proudly. Maybe she can take half the grease, he thought. The Company's got the rest. His spirits were high. Even Flynn was keeping his hands off. And then it was Friday afternoon.

"Hi." She was leaning out of the casement window, shaking her hair.

"Hi." He was looking at his scooter by streetlight. It was chained to a no-parking sign.

She threw down the key. He opened the heavy-duty padlock and locked the chain back around the sign. He turned on the ignition and pumped buttons to feed the two Solex carburetors. He closed the choke, squeezed the clutch, cracked the hand throttle, and booted the starter crank.

On the first pump the Beezer caught. The pipes echoed a sweet roar as he goosed the throttle and eased off the choke. His pulse thumped as he moved the bike upright and kicked up the side stand. The engine warmed, and he swung a leg over the frame, grazing the new sissy bar back of the saddle. He sat listening and feeling the pounding power under him. Then he turned on the lights, squeezed the clutch and rapped the foot shift. Rolling easy, he bounced down the curb and set up in the middle of West Seventy-fifth. He popped the clutch and did a wheelie that had his pipes sparking on the pavement before he came down, fifty feet from the corner candy store. He screeched to a stop at the Columbus Avenue crosswalk.

He felt the cold wind filling his body with freedom as he boomed down Columbus to Broadway, leaned into Columbus Circle and headed past the *Maine* Monument into Central Park. He rode through the park, cracking the throttle in bursts.

The Son of Man coming in a cloud with power and great glory. This he thought. This he felt. Without Carlee, he never would have had this. With Carlee, power and great glory. He headed home to her.

He chained his bike. He went up to his apartment. He took Carlee in his arms and scooped her up. He laid her down on the bed. He kicked off his shoes and lay down beside her.

"I'm all hot and smelly," he said. He fumbled.

"I don't care."

"Right."

"I love you."

"Right."

"I want to do for you. Anything. I'll do anything for you."

"Right." Even so, he couldn't give himself to her completely. The Company lurked in his mind.

18

He woke up and noticed his arm was asleep. Carlee was curled up next to him with her head on his shoulder. It was cold. She moved and opened her eyes, looking at him in the dim light.

She threw her arms around him, and it happened again.

Later still, they showered and dressed. Magically, she produced a leather jacket and well-worn boots. His eyes were grubby from sleeping with his contacts in. He fished two helmets with plastic bubble masks out of one of the kitchen cabinets.

"Not yet. Wait'll we get down."

"I just wanted to try it on."

"It'll work; let's get truckin'." He started out the door.

She was strung out behind him, holding on to the belt loop in the back of his Levis. "Thanks," she said.

"Thank yourself, Carlee."

He went through the starting ritual again. When he had the bike up and the engine thumping nice and regular, he pulled his hat over his ears. He kicked down the passenger footpegs and motioned to her to get on. She settled in and put her arms around his waist. Light she was and like a fairy, he thought.

And then they rode. Down to black Forty-second Street, with shivering hookers and lights and dark niches filled with drifters and grifters.

They wheeled across town to Fifth Avenue and roared with the synchronized streetlights down to Washington Square and Greenwich Village. Every once in a while he'd hug his elbows in to his sides, squeezing her arms, too. She'd hug him back.

She rode great, as though she'd been on bikes or horses all her life. All lean, no twist. Just her hands knotted up across his stomach to remind him that he was packing.

Then they rode onto F.D.R. Drive, heading uptown along the East River. It was clear and cold. They passed a lot of New York. They saw some. But mostly it was the feeling of the ride and just, by God, being there and doing it.

They left the Drive and turned west, crosstown. He pulled up in front of his building on West Seventy-fifth and chained the bike back to the sign.

"You're good," he said.

"You're beautiful."

"Right."

"You ride well. It was freedom."

"I know."

"Teach me?"

"Sometime."

"But I'd rather be with you on the bike."

"Right."

They walked back up to the apartment.

19

At six-thirty he awoke. He had something cooking in his mind. Carlee was little snores next to him. He wanted a cigarette. He eased out of bed and stumbled into the kitchen, closing the door behind him. He found the light switch and his Kools. The smoke made the thickness in his throat feel fine, and he took a couple of quick hits before he thought about getting something to cover up his gooseflesh.

He got a towel from the bathroom and put on his leather jacket. He hunted up a scratch pad and a pencil. And then he got a fantasy going. He plugged in his mind and lit another cigarette. Six Kools and half an hour later, he had some things to write down:

R201—a ten-mile-square area of southern Nepal with a sliver of northern India, ordered by chance.

A square storm in R201.

A cutoff of his previously unlimited right to request prints.

Flynn—butter wouldn't melt in his mouth. But he seemed straight.

The bug.

Bingo! If the office was bugged, they had heard his phone call with Carlee. He had denied meeting anyone that Friday morning on the way to work. They'd find out he had lied to the checkers from Langley. If his house was bugged, they'd know about Carlee too. If he only knew when and why the bug had gone in. S.O.P., or because he'd raised some hackles? Either way, he was probably in deep trouble, because someone was bound to figure out that he had beaten the lie detector. And that was true whether the anomaly in R201 was something sinister or just an innocent, typical, down-to-earth technological fuck-up.

"What are you writing?"

He looked up through the accumulated menthol haze and saw her, sleepy-eyed and wrapped in a comforter. She was lovely. "My will. Go back to sleep. We've got a big day."

"No, seriously, why're you up?"

"I just ordered out for a six-foot bagel and a hundred pounds of cream cheese. I'm going to Central Park Lake after the Great White Lox. Night."

"Night, night." She closed the door behind her.

Well, maybe they were put off by his Malibu madness. But now, by God, he'd better come up with something, or his ass was grass.

The question impinged on his rational self. Sanroc and the computers didn't make mistakes. They were like jet engines: once they were going, they kept on going. Only the people who programmed the computers or interpreted the results could make mistakes. The bottom line kept coming up sinister.

Then he got an idea. The logic was simple. The initial arbiter of aberrations was the N.R.O. computer itself. Each bit of information coming from Sanroc was measured against a norm for that particular area. When the original Sanroc satellite had finished the first periodic survey of the world in late 1969, every single earth sector had been printed as a C.P.R., analyzed, and then put on the computer by a huge *human* analysis staff. The process of manually establishing computer norms for the C.P.R.s had taken nearly three years.

Final norms were established, based on the original run, together with other data, such as tides, population, normal glacial movements and the like. Once completed, these norms had become the basis for comparison of all the incoming Sanroc data. Any variation from the norms as originally programmed or amended by later aberration reports produced a C.P.R. for review—the point at which Talon's job and the jobs of an unknown number of others started.

Talon's problem lay in the fact that if something in R201 was peculiar, whatever was peculiar lay under the clouds. As far as getting confirmatory information from the Company was concerned, it was out of the question, after the developments of the past several days. He added another line to his list:

Cover-up.

If there was no answer, he'd better make some alternative plans for his future life-style. He could wind up so covert that no one would hear from him again.

He added another word:

Proof.

And another:

Leads.

By eight-fifteen all he had were some scrawls and an urgent desire to get warm and happy by crawling back into bed with Carlee. Half an hour had gone by without a single cogent thought. The day looked promisingly bright, but his bedroom had lightproof curtains, which made it pleasant for sleeping in.

Then he figured that he had been attacking the lion head-on. Perhaps some working forward from the tail instead might be in order.

He pulled the phone into the bathroom. He turned on the water in the tub. Then he got the portable computer terminal out of his closet. He closed the door and set up shop. He dialed Octopus. He put the receiver on the terminal, addressed the N.R.O. computer, and typed in his personal code. Then he started querying:

Q. TIME: EST. GO.

He waited. Almost immediately the terminal translated the assorted bleeps and whistles coming in over the wire.

A. TIME: EST. 08:27. GO.

Talon nodded. So, at least at some level in the program, he was not *persona non grata*.

Q. TIME: LOS ANGELES, CALIFORNIA, USA. GO.
A. TIME: LOS ANGELES, CALIFORNIA, USA. 05:27. GO.
Q. AREA: NEW YORK CITY, NEW YORK, USA. GO.
A. AREA: NEW YORK CITY, NEW YORK, USA. 320.38 SQ MI. GO.

The terminal was chattering back the answers quickly. He continued:

Q. BIGGEST: ROCK, WORLD. GO.
A. BIGGEST: ROCK, WORLD. AYERS ROCK, AUSTRALIA. GO.
Q. SIZE: AYERS ROCK, AUSTRALIA. GO.
A. UNANSWERABLE. CHECK INPUT DATA. GO.

Smartass machine.

Q. AREA: AYERS ROCK, AUSTRALIA. GO.
A. AREA: AYERS ROCK, AUSTRALIA. 300,000 ACRES. GO.

Interesting. He'd have to remember that in case someone ever asked.

He tried to think of some more questions to move forward with. One unauthorized query and it would be like one of those Master Charge cash machines that eat the card at four in the morning when you need a quick fifty.

```
     Q. DATE FOUNDED: NEWARK, NEW JERSEY,
USA. GO.
     A. DATE FOUNDED: NEWARK, NEW JERSEY,
USA. L666. GO.
     Q. JEWISH POPULATION: L960, BROOKLYN,
NEW YORK, USA. GO.
     A. JEWISH POPULATION: L960, BROOKLYN,
NEW YORK, USA. L32,853. GO.
     Q. SHEEP POPULATION: L965, NEW
ZEALAND. GO.
     A. SHEEP POPULATION: L965, NEW
ZEALAND. 6L,283,000. GO.
     Q. AREA: CULTIVATED LANDS, NEPAL. GO.
```

He held his breath.

```
     A. AREA: CULTIVATED LANDS, NEPAL.
4,524,6L5 ACRES. GO.
     Q. LANGUAGE: NEPAL. GO.
     A. LANGUAGE: NEPAL. NEPALI (CALLED
ALSO HURKHALI, KHASKURA, PARBATIYA). GO.
```

He continued, hoping that he could work into and through
the areas he needed information on, without tripping the
cutoff to his access. He figured the cutoff had to be
programmed into Octopus.

```
     Q. POPULATION: NEPAL. GO.
     A. POPULATION: NEPAL. L2,572,000
(L975 ESTIMATE). GO.
```

He was thinking about how he could edge into questions
which might have some probative value. His phone bill was
going to be horrendous.

```
     Q. ROAD: NEPAL BORDER TERMINUS
POINTS, INDIA TO CHINA. GO.
```

He held his breath. In 1967, India had built a road through
Nepal to the Chinese border in what had once been Tibet.

70

The military and political consequences of that road were fairly staggering, and Nepal, by outlawing the Communist party, had reduced the exposures not one iota. So, without regard as to how the square storm had magically appeared on R201, assuming, arguendo, for the sake of the fifty percent of Talon that had an immortal soul, that it was not some basic mechanical error, the road was a logical sore point.

If it was, the computer didn't seem to care.

```
A. ROAD: NEPAL BORDER TERMINUS
POINTS, INDIA TO CHINA. NEPAL BORDER
SOUTH; NEPAL BORDER NORTH. GO.
```

He tried other sensitive areas in addressing the computer. He queried the computer with respect to the personnel in Nepal's Legat office, and, since Legat is the foreign branch of the FBI, he expected a shutdown. He got an answer.

He queried about exchange rates and dollar volume. The Company played fast and loose with big bucks in foreign exchange; maybe that was the sensitive point. Wrong again.

Nepal is more than a beautiful land. It sits in a very sensitive position astride the Himalayas between the two most populous countries in the world. Discouragement started coming in in spades as the terminal rapped out what seemed to be reams of highly classified answers on the accordion IBM paper. He was having trouble coming up with more general questions involving secret matters from which he might be excluded.

So he went to the photo areas. First he addressed the computer's memory specifically on S201, R's neighbor. He asked about crops, cloud cover, rainfall, a five-year history of aberrations. He asked about military significance, oil and timber. He asked about animal life, flooding and altitude. He couldn't think of anything more. All his questions were answered, based on stored factual information and observations, the original world survey and its follow-ups over the years. No problem.

He held his breath and pushed the same questions for
R201. Answered. But what answers. His heart started going
faster, and he knew he had something.

```
    A. R20L, CLOUD COVER AVG. 365 DAYS:
PERCENT 100. GO.
    A. R20L, ABERRATION REPORTS 5 YEARS:
NONE. GO.
```

Cloud cover in the adjacent S201 sector showed twenty-
three percent. In almost any area some cloud cover could be
expected. But total cover meant that Sanroc could never see.
And therefore there could never be an aberration-report
request kicked out of the computer. Total cover would be the
norm. Impossible. The norm was wrong and the C.P.R. was
wrong. Impossible.

He sat and explored the facts. The data-bank report of
cloud cover showed one hundred percent. Every cycle.
Sanroc, then, had to have been sending a total-cover picture
for the weekly analysis, week in, week out, for all these
years. Therefore, no aberrations for all these years. It was not
possible, except for the fact that he had seen one example of
the transmission.

He made notes. Why? That was the easiest. Something was
under that cloud that shouldn't be there. How? Impossible to
put together right away. It would take the manufacture of a
permanent cloud. Impossible. Or . . . Later. Assuming he was
right, what was there? He'd have to find an atlas and get
some other information.

He started to query the computer on specifics for the R201
area. They all came up snake eyes. Nothing. Absolutely
nothing. He gave up and signaled the end of his queries to
the computer. It went bye bye. Talon listened to the
whistling outer-space sound of Octopus for a moment from
the receiver. Then he hung up. Then he started to think
about himself.

His closet held a lot of potentially damning gear. It was

time to start cleaning up the rest of his act and getting some cover for his precious ass. Sooner or later someone might be interested in searching his place.

20

"I've been waiting half an hour."

"Huh?"

"I mean, I know you're my landlord. But enough is enough." She had put her beautiful, sleepy head into the partially open bathroom doorway.

"Right. I'll be through right away."

"You sure?"

"Right."

"You feeling okay?"

"Right."

"Okay." The door closed.

"You always type in the john? With the phone?" He heard her through the door. He turned off the tap. She'd probably blown it. Certainly, if the apartment was bugged.

He had an idea how these things worked. They wouldn't have a full-time operative on him, he thought. Maybe some kind of sound-actuated recorder somewhere. Probably. Then, every so often, someone would pick up the tapes, and someone would listen to them, and someone would get down the assorted juicy parts in notes. Unless he was nuts.

But if they had the apartment bugged, they'd know he was doing something strange in the bathroom. And maybe someone would catch on to what it was. Time was not on his side, he figured. He could wait or move. So he decided to move.

"I'm going to go in the kitchen sink!" Her head was back in.

"Right. Just a second." They'd put it all together. In just a while they'd hit. Even the polygraph frolic. He could be in real trouble. And it was only ten forty-five Saturday morning. He put the top on the terminal and set it behind the door. The only question was how much time he had. He stood up, opened the door and saw her sitting on the sink.

"I warned you."

"Right."

"That's all."

"Right," he said.

"You're not mad at me?"

"Right."

"Right?"

"I love you." Who said that? He wanted to look around. But he knew it had come from him.

"Of course you do."

"Right."

"If it bothers you, you don't have to say it again." She shifted uncomfortably in her bathrobe. "Please turn around so I can get down. I'll drip dry."

"Right." He turned and took her in his arms after looking away. She turned in to him and became very small. She faced up and kissed his neck. They made some noises at each other. He felt a little weak. "Okay, shower up. We're going riding." He took the terminal out of the bathroom.

"'Grrreat,' said Tony the Tiger."

"Right."

She disappeared into the bathroom. He went to the front hall closet and got out a large Samsonite two-suiter. Then he went to his closet and started packing some gear.

He put in the checks and checkwriter, his own passport and another he'd appropriated from an old surfing buddy who'd been staying with him the year before. He packed his

Armalite rifle and accessories. He boxed some stationery and packed it. He packed everything else that might look suspicious to a searcher, including his grass. Paranoid. He thought about what he was doing and got a little sick to his stomach. The thought of Monday made him sicker. Also, sometime he would have to tell Carlee the facts. Now he had to; no way around it. Barf.

He opened his phone book and got the number for the Hilton. He called and secured agreement from the desk to hold his luggage for a couple of days.

He filled up the suitcase with some more of his closet gear. A closet cretin, he thought. He closed the suitcase and lugged it to the door. He went back and got the portable terminal. He heard the shower going.

"I'll be back in about half an hour," he yelled through the bathroom door.

He heard a muffled reply. He lugged the two large cases downstairs and out to the sidewalk, where the scooter was sitting. A miracle of poetry, he thought. It was shining and beautiful in the morning haze. Powerful-looking. All chromy and black.

Leave the cases, grab Carlee, throw a leg over that sweet little mother, and scoot out of town, he heard a voice in his ear saying. Run, do not walk, to the nearest exit. Crack out of this doodoo-littered wilderness and head back to the beach.

Can't, he said to himself as he hailed a cab. Those fantasies were lived once, and the perfect wave rolled by ten years ago. He yelled "Hilton!" through the plexiglass protector between him and the driver. Screw 'em, he thought ten minutes later, when he checked the cases with one of the bellhops at the baggage room. Monday would be his last check-in with Flynn.

21

"Where'd you go?"

"To say goodbye to all my other women."

"It didn't take very long."

"I gave a collective farewell address at Yankee Stadium."

"Hold them all?"

"Lots of seats on the infield."

"Oh." She was wrapped in a towel and crowned with another. Goosefleshy and grinning.

"Let's get going, woman. It's eleven-fifteen, and we've got a lot of ground to cover."

"Places to go and people to see."

"Right."

"Well, I'd better get cracking."

"Right."

Within five minutes she appeared, magically shining and glowing, five feet of smile stretched out across her face. She was toting a blue nylon knapsack.

"Panties and makeup."

"Right."

"And some other odds and ends."

"Not many." He picked up a tie-top canvas bag and a couple of shock cords. "Go on down; I'll be with you in a minute, after I lock up."

As soon as she left, he pulled the phone over and set it by the door. He lifted the receiver slightly. He put a pencil under it to keep the receiver from touching the disconnect buttons. He opened the door and took his gear. With the door nearly closed, he reached in and nudged the phone around so that the floor bar for the high-security door lock would not clear the pencil. He closed the door, then opened it again.

The bar had knocked the pencil from the phone, and the receiver was back on the hook.

He reset the pencil and went through the procedure again. This time he locked up. He dialed his number from the hallway pay phone. It was busy.

Brilliant, he thought. Another telltale for those goons from Langley. Well, fuck 'em. If they want to take away my privacy, the sanctity of my house, at least I'll know about it.

22

"Here, take that sack off," he said. "I'll hang it on the sissy bar."

"That's great."

"And I'll just hook my old canvas bag on with these here spring cords. Just panties and makeup."

"Right." She giggled.

"You know, you can just lean back. You don't have to hold so tight."

"Sure, but I want to." She looked determined.

"Right."

"Where are we going, master?"

"The grand tour."

The day was doing its March thing in New York, with general clarity and specific cloud cover. It promised coolness, the possibility of showers and the probability of light traffic.

"The Island," he said.

"Long?"

"Right." He kicked the engine over and it fired. "Mount up."

She bumped her clear-plastic face mask against his and kissed him through it. They both laughed and got aboard.

They cleared West Seventy-fifth Street, leaning and turning on avenues and crosstown streets, whipping across the Park. They headed downtown on Fifth, mirrored in the crystal-clear plate glass of Tiffany, Saks and Gennori. The Brando of the haute monde, he was rapping his pipes, echoes lifting up the escarpment to the Top of the Sixes. On the run downtown to the Battery, he felt the secret world of Talon One slipping away. The more acceptable aspects of Talon Two in the schizoid bi-level of his life gained reality. His frenetic mental preparations for career disaster—and worse—lost some importance. He put them away for later.

He felt her front against his back, and the world went by. It was shiver-good. The Beezer kept pumping out that mellow throb. The occasional unavoidable New York chuckhole was the only shocking reminder of reality, throwing a kidney into orbit and cracking Carlee's helmet against his.

Time to think. Time to dream. He rode with a careful mind and eye. Defensive. Most of the traffic flowed light, but the cabs came fast. Nobody likes a biker, he thought. Detroit iron constantly threatened to graze the vulnerable space through which Talon and Carlee hurtled. He'd lived with that threat all the years of freedom the bike had given to him.

T. E. Lawrence had gone south that way, he reflected. All that camel shit, Turks, and shooting. Then Lawrence had made hamburger out of himself and a ball out of his scooter right in his own backyard. A death wish?

He started backing himself into the death-wish mode.

Number one, everyone knew that kicking a big old scooter around was pushing the odds on the mortality table. Number two, the adventure fantasies played those funny tunes in his head.

Number three waited a moment as he set up and hit an enormous pit at Twenty-third Street. No avoiding it.

"Oof," he heard Carlee say. No gripes.

Number three, he thought, it's the way Talon gets things done. Nothing had a simple, everyday solution. The shit always had to hit the fan.

No. Impossible. He took the big risk, but it was all *mano a mano*. Waiting to go in over the horns and wearing a flak jacket. He decided that, unlike Lawrence, he enjoyed the occasional roll in the hay and the fantasy of a Carlee too much to take the deep six easily. He would not go gentle into that good night.

The musing ended as he found himself at the Brooklyn Battery Tunnel. He made it through, gagging at the exhaust fumes. He pulled over at the Brooklyn end and got some air.

"Okay?" he yelled through the helmet to Carlee.

"Sure. I've been dreaming and looking and loving it. Except for the tear gas in the tunnel."

"If any of those idiots start crawling up my back, don't be afraid to let me know."

"Sure will, Joe."

He cranked the bike again and headed south on the Expressway, through scenic Brooklyn, and picked up the Shore Parkway along Gravesend Bay. He exited at the Coney Island sign. He took a quick look around to make sure nothing was drifting loose.

"Bikes vibrate like crazy. Got to keep checking things out; they'll shake down to a basket of bolts quick if you don't watch out," he said.

After a quick pit stop at a friendly gas station, they were on the road again, heading east, picking up the Belt Parkway.

Traffic was okay, the air was clearer, and Carlee was doing her hugging thing. They passed the wild Jamaica Bay flats with their stinking water and Canarsie Beach Park. Jets from J.F.K. screamed overhead. Talon stopped again to firm up directions. Then, just before clearing the city limits, Talon noticed flashing lights behind him. He pulled over and stopped. He put down the kickstand, and off they got. The cop wasn't moving, so Talon walked back.

"Yes, officer?" Butter wouldn't melt.

"Driver's license and registration, please."

Talon fumbled at his wallet. "What's the story? For once I was right on the dot. The double nickel. Fifty-five?"

"The papers, sir."

Sir didn't come out California-style. For sure, the beefy boy in blue and his twin brother had never meant sir in their lives. Must be Be Polite to Citizens Week. Talon finally located the required documents in his wallet and handed them over. He glanced up and saw Carlee pacing around. Embarrassed. It's easier to hide when you get a ticket in a car, he thought.

The cop started scribbling at his ticket book immediately. Tweedledee looked blank and bored in the car. Talon decided not to engage either of them in idle conversation, although curiosity was killing him.

When he had finished with the writing, the cop shuffled to Talon's registration and squinted at the license plate. Then he heaved himself out of the car and walked over to the bike. Talon noticed that the sag of the squad car's front seat matched the cop's massive hindquarters. Comfy.

"Nice scooter." He stooped to look for the motor number.

A kindred soul? Yet so porcine? "Other side, Serpico."

Not a twitch. "Thank you, sir."

Same sir. Sarcastic. "So what's coming down? If I may be so bold. I mean I'm starting to feel a communication gap."

"Sir," the cop said again, looking up with cunning eyes

and a reflective cast to his globular face, "one more smartass scumbag remark, and you will be wearing this scooter and bleeding a lot. Sir."

"Right." Obviously a Mexican standoff.

Numbers checked, the cop courteously handed Talon the ticket, license and registration. All business. Then he drove away.

"I made their whole day," Talon said.

"What happened?"

"It says 'taillight obscured.'"

"That's right. My pack slipped down." She pointed.

"Ah well, no matter, my dear. I shall adjust it, and we'll be off. A display of metropolitan jejunity, what? All aflutter about nothing. No matter."

23

At six-thirty, under a dark sky, they wheeled into Montauk. He was tired. His rear was pins and needles. Even though the ride had been highway most of the way, the constant vibration, noise and concentration had taken their toll. He knew she was wrecked, too.

A search of the quiet streets produced a clapboard rooming house. It looked as though it should be inexpensive. He stopped the bike and turned it off. He kicked down the stand and they dismounted.

"Whew!"

"Right."

"I've got a headache."

"Right."

"It was wonderful, but my ears are still ringing."

"Right." He could just barely hear the clicks and snaps from the cooling engine. His head felt stuffed. It was wonderful.

"I may have permanently impaired my female equipment. It's the first time since I met you that I'm numb."

"You'll be fine. Let's see if we can get a place to rest the weary bones. Leave the gear on the bike, and we'll present a less obtrusive front."

"Okay." She started up the drive to the house.

"The helmet."

"After a whole day, it's like part of my head."

They left the helmets next to the bike and walked to the door.

Carlee paved the way. The proprietor didn't take his eyes off her tired body, even when Talon came riding up the drive.

The second-floor room was adequate, clean and cool. Carlee was in the bath before Talon got the gear upstairs. Talon One had a moment, and he went down to the pay phone to call his apartment. Busy.

As he labored up the steps, he got to thinking that the seven-odd years of schizophrenia had pushed him off the deep end. One thing for sure, he was going to seriously rethink his life plan.

Halfway to his room he saw the proprietor and requested a wake-up call in two hours. Then he showered and moved into bed to join Carlee, who was already sleeping.

When they woke, they vaguely remembered some knocking, some groans and vows to snooze only for another fifteen minutes. They lay there, late-morning sun streaming in the window. Just a little maple-floored room with adjoining bath. Lots of chintz and lady things. Simple.

"That's you, Joe. The only thing I know about you is that I love you."

"Love. L-U-S-T spells love."

"That's right. I want you. With me. Sharing and rolling around. But something's missing, I can tell."

"Right."

"No. Tell me."

"I said, right. You are."

"Well, then, what's missing?"

"Half of me. A me I don't even know."

"What are you saying? I don't understand."

"It's part of the riddle. Part of the insanity. We'll play today. Tonight we roll home, and then I tell all."

They took showers, and he went down to phone home again. Still busy. He felt even more sure that he had overreacted.

24

That clear afternoon they rode to the old Montauk lighthouse, sniffed at the sea breeze and watched the gulls. They looked at the boats in the harbor, party boats, with amateur fishermen dangling catches of porgy, blues, flounder and fluke; clam boats, commercial fishers, sailboats, outboard prams. People working on them or gawking at them.

"Want one, Joe?"

"In some movie, Shirley MacLaine, I think, said, 'I can't take care of a Chiclet.' That's the way I feel. If you have a three-foot boat, the front two feet need work before you can get to the back one."

"Sailing with me?"

"Now, that changes the direction the cool wind blows, my dear. With you at the helm and me sick over the rail . . ."

She poked him. "You'd never get sick. It's like a big surfboard."

"Right." He remembered the time he almost had.

"We could sail to Tahiti."

"Right." He remembered the time he almost had. He wanted to tell her they would. He didn't.

"Or we could just stay in the harbor and make waves."

"That's better."

They walked and looked. They held hands and bumped into each other. Sometimes they stopped and kissed.

"We had better head back. It's almost dark now."

"Thanks, Joe. I'll never forget this."

"Me either."

"I'm glad you didn't say 'right.' That's good."

"Right."

She gave him a big hug and kiss.

25

On a summer Sunday evening, it would be murder coming in from the Island. Magnetic New York, drawing in all the share people from Fire Island, Amagansett, and the Hamptons, mixing them with the day people from Lido, Long Beach, and Rockaway. The summer weekend rush hour. But not in March. The road that night was clear.

They had on extra sweaters. Carlee bumped tiredly against him as they rode down the center of Long Island on the

Expressway. It was no sightseeing trip. But it was faster than the Brooklyn route. He knew she'd be half dozing. The misery of discomfort on a bike was an acquired taste.

She stirred against him as it got colder toward ten o'clock. He pulled onto the shoulder at Roslyn and shut down the bike.

"Let's walk for a couple of minutes."

"Okay." She dismounted. "I'm a little tired."

"That's okay, Carlee. It's just hard to keep the wheels on the road if you move around. We'll be warm in bed in forty-five minutes. So try to keep awake. Wide awake."

"All right." She looked like she might be tired-pouty, but she kept it together.

"Thanks." He gave her hand a big squeeze. "You're a great sport."

They wheeled back onto the highway. He gritted his teeth against the weather, the road shocks and the vibrations. He loved it.

He was loving it when he crossed the New York City line and was still loving it two miles later when Carlee shrieked in his ear, twisted on the saddle, and upset the delicate balance of the bike. It slewed at sixty miles an hour directly across the left lane, over the shoulder and onto a dirt slope. Talon saw a black shape hurtle by, no lights showing, as he fought by easy stages to pick an acceptable straight-line path. Carlee was crushing him in a desperate bear hug. For a sickening split second they were airborne over a ditch; then they came back onto the highway, with the wheels still under them.

Adrenaline-loaded blood was pumping through his body. He saw the shadow again, a black car weaving just ahead but slowing down. He needed to yell for help. The guy was a nut. They would have been chopped liver if Carlee hadn't panicked.

He spotted a slow-moving van in the right lane ahead. The

black car was now only a few yards in front of them. As it started to come at them across lanes, Talon dropped his bike into third and screamed up the shoulder to the right of the van, leaving both behind. He glanced back and caught the black car coming fast. Holy shit, he thought, the crazy bastard is still behind me. At eighty-five he shifted up to fourth and kept the throttle wide open. The rear-view mirror was vibrating so much it was useless.

He wondered how fast the other guy could go. Where were those twin blue bastards now? Never there when you need them. The B.S.A. was now flat-out at one hundred and fifteen, give or take a bit. Up ahead, a clot of cars was spread across the road. Carlee, darlin', don't move that pretty butt of yours a centimeter. He headed straight for them.

The wind was devastating. He couldn't turn his head at all now to look, for fear the plastic bubble mask would rip right off. He needed it.

He picked the space between the center and left-lane cars. Right on the lane-divider line, he whipped between them, fighting for control and cool.

He slowed to eighty and checked over his shoulder. Nothing. He slowed to fifty, then to forty, figuring on hanging out in front of those people until the world got better. He took a sweet, banked turn onto the Brooklyn–Queens Expressway, northbound to the Triborough Bridge. There were always cops there. He checked over his shoulder; still nothing.

He didn't see the second black car until it was too late, when it sideswiped him. The driver of that one had a really fine angle on the bike.

Talon fought the good fight, but it was no go. The bike left the road and the shoulder, headed up a steep embankment and did a backward one-eighty. Scrap. They stayed on most of the way, then they flew.

Talon relaxed before he hit. It wasn't all that bad, he thought. He saw Carlee, a few feet away, like a Salvation Army counter doll. She looked wasted. He felt sick.

He tried to collect his strength. He heard the black car braking, then backing. He wished he'd been more regular with his meditations. He needed every ounce of whatever mental strength he could muster. And who knew how much it could have added. The bike started burning big. Goodbye, old friend.

He was lying on his back on a cobblestoned incline. He could see the backup lights of the black car coming right up toward him. He concentrated on Aikido breathing. Long, quiet, even breaths, in to that single spot in his lower abdomen, then out to heaven, pouring forth the universal *ki*. Aikido, the martial art with the spirit of love, the spirit of protection for all things. He concentrated on his unbendable arm, on his own unbreakable spirit.

As the car backed over him, Talon rolled over once. The wheel just grazed his shoulder. He heard the driver shift to park, and the backup lights went out. This was murder. The bastard is crazy. Wild thoughts of fear and escape threatened to break into the Zen peacefulness Talon knew he must retain in order to cope.

The door of the car opened over Talon. With infinite love and protection he caught the driver in the thigh with a kick. The kick had *ki*, the indefinable, and it poured forth from the toe of Talon's riding boot to the point of contact. The driver screamed with the pain and made a move to lay hands on Talon. Again the concentration and *ki*. This time Talon's toe found the man's throat. No sound. The man toppled back into the car.

Talon felt nothing as he willed himself to his feet. Carlee had not moved. The bike was ablaze twenty feet away, tires sending black smoke swirling about, choking him.

Carlee's pack and his canvas bag were part of the litter. He picked his up and looked at her again. He couldn't stand it. He touched her slim neck: nothing.

The driver hadn't moved. Talon was sure he wouldn't. He pushed the man farther over in the seat. Then Talon backed the car over the fire and got out.

He heard a car coming but didn't see lights. Terrific. He wanted to run, but he only managed a game hobble up to the top of the embankment. He dropped flat. The death car's tires started burning as he rolled under a chain-link fence.

He looked back and saw a coat-and-tie man get out of the other car, run over to the first car and look in the window. He got in on the driver's side. The car started rolling down the embankment. It was about twenty feet from the burning bike when the gas tank blew up.

Talon walked. He wanted only two things—distance and a pay phone. The image of his broken lady was all he could see. He felt great anger. Sorrow would come later. His eyes cried.

Every siren in New York was wailing. Where are they when you need 'em. It was an answer, not a question. Nowhere.

He started hurting. The extra sweater had cushioned his fall a bit. Aikido had helped. The helmet had saved his head and face. He started a physical self-appraisal. He had some sticking pains in his back when he took a breath, and he wasn't functioning with a great deal of sensory clarity. His neck hurt. His head hurt.

He unbuckled the helmet and pulled it off. It was cracked at the back like an eggshell. Exactly what the fiberglass is supposed to do, dissipate the shock. Could have fooled me, he thought. The inside of the hat was sticky with blood. His right ear was bleeding. Concussion. He chucked the hat into an alley. Exhibit A.

He thought about a fractured skull. *Que sera sera.* He didn't want to move. He kept putting one foot in front of the other. They kept working. Time, hung up on a grease rack. Five minutes ago, there was life. Now, death.

He came to a pay phone outside a dark candy store. Everything else was a haze. He dialed his home phone. It rang and rang. Anger raged with pain.

Farther along he found himself walking over a bridge. He looked down and saw a lot of railroad tracks. He scrambled down the abutment and under the bridge. He found a spot next to the rails, lay down in the gravel roadbed, put his head on his canvas bag, and passed out.

The rush and roar in his ears was horrendous as he suddenly awoke. A freight train was moving by at a reasonably fast clip. The danger was minimal. The noise, though, was shattering, even with his hands clapped over his ears. It shut out another kind of pain. He had no place to go. No one. Carlee. He wanted the train to roll forever, an infinite number of cars making an infinite amount of noise, so he could lie there and not have to think about what to do next, so the ground could shake him and let him know why he trembled.

It did last a long time, the noise, the rumbling, the rush of air about him. And then it ended. The train had scared him. He looked at his watch. It was stopped at the time death had come. Then the horror flooded into his conscious mind. This terrible thing could not have happened to him. But it had, and the sense it made, the logic of how he had killed Carlee, engulfed him.

He had trouble standing. His contact lenses were glued to his corneas. He felt nauseated. His head hurt, and breathing produced more of the sticking pain. He hitched his canvas bag over his shoulder and started trudging along the tracks.

He felt like a bum. A tramp. He'd stepped into a bear trap. And now he was track-walking. The call he had made to his home seemed so far away in time. He wasn't positive he had made it. But the hell that he faced was tied in with it. They were looking for him. To kill him. He knew nothing, but the sensitivity of what he had done on the computer would mean death to him. Had already meant death to Carlee.

He trudged on and on. A Medusa-Tinkerbell of reality flitted about his head, dropping pain and guilt. And he walked some more.

There were four sets of rails. He walked the roadbed until his feet ached from fighting the gravel, then he started to walk the ties. The thought of being converted into mush by a train didn't cross his mind. Just anger and sorrow.

The roadbed started rising. It became a trestle, the long approach to the bridge spanning the treacherous Hell Gate channel between Randall's Island and the Borough of Queens. The tides rushing through the East River between Long Island Sound and New York Harbor produce powerful currents and whirlpools at the Hell Gate. Hulks of ships line its boneyard bottom.

Talon began to feel the physical pain of his body and the wracking depression of Carlee's death. Then the roadbed disappeared as he walked the ties on an elevated structure. He could look down to the dim street, fifty or sixty feet below. He saw the long stretch of trestle and bridge ahead. He thought about dodging a train and falling between the ties. Now he felt fear.

The trestle kept rising. So did his discomfort. He stopped and took a couple of pennies from his pocket. He found a rail split—a place where the rails were not joined by bolted gussets. Instead, the rail sections were insulated from each other. A train going over this point would complete an electrical circuit and trip signals to prevent collisions.

He placed a penny over each of the splits, bridging the gaps. He saw red signal lights go on. A ghost train. Until someone found and removed the pennies, he'd be safe walking between the two rails. He plodded on over the Hell Gate, from tie to tie, with the dark waters rushing beneath.

26

"I guess you'd better call the security people from Langley again," said Flynn.

"I don't like that smartass, and I never did. Every morning that 'Moneypenny' stuff."

"I can't say that I care for him in some ways. But overall, he is a fine, quick reader with a brilliant mind and a rather fascinating personality."

"I think he's a witless dodo. Always tweeking someone's beak. That's all he's good for, Mr. Flynn." Miss D'Arcy thrust out an indignant chest. "I'll call. Every week, and a general alarm goes out. He's probably hungover and sweated up in some bimbo's bed." She dialed and huffed at the same time.

"Are you sure *you* don't want a piece of him?" Flynn reached out to her and squeezed a nipple between his thumb and forefinger. Hard.

She placed the receiver back on the cradle and cupped the breast with her hand. She rolled her eyes back and started breathing audibly. So did Flynn. "You old dog." The signal.

"You bitch." He stood up.

She breathed harder. "Yes."

"Bitch." He squeezed more.

"Yes." She cupped more and snaked her other hand under her dress. She didn't believe in panties. She started moving around.

He pulled his hand away. "On your knees."

She dropped to her knees, awkwardly, keeping her fingers

in place between her legs. She unzipped his pants with her free hand and pulled him out.

He edged forward to help. And they finished off together in a quaking tableau of grunts.

He pushed her away and rearranged himself. "Maybe if Talon gave you some once in a while, you'd feel different."

She reached for him again.

"Not now, Miss D'Arcy." He sat and took the growl out of his voice. "Please make the call."

27

The pro crew from Langley arrived two hours later. Miss D'Arcy led them into Flynn's office.

"Talon again, huh?" Blue said.

"Yes. I'm sure it's just another of his hungover mornings."

"He is an expensive piece of business. We have more pressing places to spend time and money. He's just part of the contract labor force," said Blue. He liked to do the talking.

"He puts out five times what my next best does. He's worth it."

"Does he know it?"

"I told him. I said twice what the others did."

"When?"

"Last week."

"Gone to his head?"

Miss D'Arcy decided to volunteer. "He arranged his carrel, first time ever."

"Coop cleanin', huh?" said Gray. The southern accent crept through.

"Migrating?" wondered Blue.

Flynn looked thoughtful. Miss D'Arcy looked pleased.

"Let's check the nest," said Blue.

Flynn and Miss D'Arcy each took out a key, and they used them to open a safe-deposit-type box in a cupboard behind Flynn's desk. Miss D'Arcy reached into the box and removed the duplicate Medoc key to Talon's carrel.

"Let's see what our bird's up to," said Blue, taking the key.

"This isn't an aviary," said the prim Miss D'Arcy.

"You have your fun; we'll have ours," said Blue.

Miss D'Arcy did one of her holier-than-thou scarlet acts.

Flynn glanced at his fly and looked up to find Blue and Gray staring at him.

Miss D'Arcy led the way, with the two men from Langley behind her.

"Where's the stuff he threw out?" said Gray.

"Except for a stack of computer photos, it's all gone. There was just garbage. Old sandwiches, papers, roaches."

"Roaches, here?" said Blue.

"New York is the universal roach convention center."

"You're a fount of information, ma'am. I was referring, however, to the pristine environment of this office."

"Oh."

They let themselves in.

"If the bird has flown," Blue said, "we'd want to know where. Don't you think?"

Blue and Gray started to demolish the office. They went through everything.

"Nice setup," said Gray.

"Umph," said Blue, as he started to move the carrel furniture around.

"Cleaning up was a bit out of character, I take it," said Gray.

"Yes, definitely," said Miss D'Arcy.

"As security chief, I take it you had no interest in the matter," said Blue.

"Well . . ."

"I mean, when somebody is going to fly, doesn't it make sense to let us know?" said Blue.

"Don't get testy."

"Look, it's in the job description. Why no report?"

"He just wasn't the type to run."

Exasperation climaxed, and he took a deep breath. "Yours is not to wonder why. The standard operating procedure is that when there's a change in a man, we ask questions. Simple."

"I didn't consider it a change, and . . ."

"Hey, look at this," said Gray. With his southern drawl, he immediately stood out from the eastern-establishment Company men, which was probably why he didn't talk much. He pointed under the desk.

"A bug?" asked Miss D'Arcy.

"Jesus!" said Blue. "Holy Christ! You dumb bitch."

She felt a bit of dampness and started to look interested.

"Who the hell got you into this job?" he wanted to know. "I mean, if I ever saw such a display of goddamn stupidity. . ." He ranted for another minute before pulling Miss D'Arcy and Gray from the carrel. He closed the door.

"Miss D'Arcy, you have blown, maybe, any chance we may have had to find out *who* is listening. You should have kept your mouth shut. The whole affair stinks. You are incompetent!"

"Don't yell. I'm standing right here."

"Don't change the subject! You are dumb, and I don't care about your goddamn tits, so quit waving them!"

Definitely wet, she thought. "I have to go to the ladies' room. If you gentlemen will excuse me for a few minutes?" She walked away.

"Goddamn cunt," said Blue, without caring that she

heard. She walked a bit faster. "Why don't you go get the electronic gear? I'll rustle around in here, just in case no one's heard." He was exasperated. "Who would be bugging some contract eyeball?"

"We don't have a car."

"Here's ten dollars. Okay? Take a cab. And see if you can get hold of the photos she was talking about. Ask Flynn." Blue went back into the carrel and really started to root. As he looked, he lined up the procedures in his mind. It was already one-thirty. Talon had not been seen since a little after five on Friday. He could have been anywhere on earth for a day by now. But with what? The guy was only an eyeball.

As soon as his mind got organized, Blue stopped looking and started writing. Things to do and questions to ask. Call: State to find out whether Talon had a passport, embassies for visas, airlines, Motor Vehicle Bureau for auto, his home, neighbors, Flynn, D'Arcy, relatives, girlfriends, boyfriends (?), old friends, new friends, enemies, Company personnel history, I.R.S., credit bureaus, hobbies, past employers, safe-deposit box, reading habits, religious preference, schooling, divorce, children, insurance policies, New York State tax returns.

He paused and stretched. Then he continued. Photos, Selective Service history, doctor, dentist, hospitals, police, bank accounts, car-rental agencies, political affiliations.

Shit, he thought, it was endless. He tried to recall any other areas from the Brookings Institute manual *Where's What*. Blue had studied that book at Langley for just this type of situation. Funny for the Company to have done the work for Brookings. After all, the manual is for the internal use of U.S. Government agencies.

More, he thought. Court records, newspapers, long-distance phone records, census information sheet, credit cards, fraternal organizations.

Enough. He starred the most critical areas and set the page

aside. He started going over the room again. Flynn walked in.

"Hi."

Chipper bastard, Blue thought. "Hi," he said and put a forefinger to his lips. Where was that bitch?

"Huh?"

Dumb bastard. Blue motioned to the door, and they stepped into the hall. "The room is bugged."

"Huh?"

"A bug. A listening device."

"How?"

"Under the desk."

"No, I mean how did it get here?"

"Mr. Flynn, you do your job; we'll do ours. So, just don't say anything in there, okay? I want you to look around and tell me *outside* whether anything is missing. Okay?"

"Okay."

"Fine; let's go back in."

Flynn looked around while Blue finished the order of priorities on his list. Flynn eventually handed him a note saying "nothing," and left.

Miss D'Arcy showed up trundling a stack of Computer Photo Remakes on a dolly. She looked well rested. She was sincerely annoyed when Blue asked her to find him a place to work, order him some lunch, he didn't care what, and then leave. She showed him the door of an adjacent carrel and huffed off to get the key.

He surveyed his notes one more time and looked at his watch. Two-twenty. Christ, I can't get moving, he thought. She came back with the key and promised to have his lunch shortly.

Then he got to work. First he checked the new carrel. It was clean. Then he rolled the dolly in and put the pictures on a work table. He pushed the dolly back into the hall.

Then he started phoning. And he collected a lot of

information right off. From the Motor Vehicle Bureau he got Talon's I.D. number and some initial statistics. He wrote:

Name: Joseph Barry Talon
Address: 48 W. 75th Street, N.Y.C.
License number: 104-30-5901
Color of hair: Light brown
Color of eyes: Blue
Restrictions: Corrective lenses required
Height: 6'–1"
Age: 37

He drew a blank on automobile registration. He called the Company's New York office, gave them the basic profile information, and got a girl from the secretarial pool to call the metropolitan-area hospitals. No sense chasing the goose. He wrote down her name and said he'd call back. Maybe Talon was just sick, hurt, or dead. Blue doubted it. The cleanup and the bug were just too much coincidence.

Blue stretched. He was of medium height, stocky, had had an Ivy League scholarship. He had been a ranking college wrestler in the light-heavyweight ranks. He looked it. He was dull, dedicated, and forty-eight, well out of the unfortunate happenings of Vietnam and Watergate, and thankful for it.

Not a Mellon, Lodge, Cabot or other old-school boy, he didn't quite qualify for the clubby inside at the Company. But then again, if he'd had one of those names, it would have been unthinkable to direct him to take care of a problem like Talon.

He turned on the teletype terminal, dialed Octopus and requested Talon's composite work history and security-clearance reports. The machine started printing as Gray walked in with two large aluminum suitcases.

28

"How ya doin'?" asked Gray.

"Just really starting. You're late." He hated that damn drawl.

"Traffic."

"Well, get the frequency of the bug. It's probably broadcast-band FM. But maybe it'll tell us something. Sweep the rest of this place. Let me know. Then come back, okay?"

"Sure thing," Gray drawled. He was a bit taller than Blue, ten years younger, and just as waspy-looking. He was a graduate of Texas A & M and of the Seals in Vietnam. He looked physically stronger than Blue. But they were both tough. Tough as hell.

Blue called State and found that Talon had a passport, application made in 1974 at New York. He was promised messenger delivery of a copy of the photo within two hours. He made an addition to his list:

Birthplace: Palo Alto, California

He called the New York office again and got the same girl.

"Miss Shiffler?"

"Yes. I'm sorry. I've contacted every public hospital in the five boroughs. You would not believe how many there are. I'm halfway through the private ones. Nothing yet."

"Please keep trying. Can you work late?"

"Sure."

"I've got some more."

"Go ahead. I take shorthand."

"His birthplace is Palo Alto, California. That's near San Francisco."

"Okay."

"Find out what hospital. Give it to the San Francisco office if necessary. They're three hours behind us, so it won't be too much of a problem. This is most urgent. You have the birthdate. I want any information from the birth certificate you don't have on the list of available data I gave you."

"Yes. I have all the information you gave me before. But wouldn't you have all that birth information on something else?"

Everybody's an expert. "Just do it, okay? And get back to me with the information."

By six-thirty that evening, Blue had accumulated a voluminous profile of Talon. Most information areas were neatly filled in. More data was coming in all the time. He arranged to have Miss Shiffler take over the flow. She arrived, escorted by Miss D'Arcy, as Gray returned from his sweepdown.

Blue sat Miss Shiffler down and showed her what to do, with Miss D'Arcy hovering over the proceedings. He wanted to be rid of that fluff in the worst way. But she was the security officer for this operation.

He left the carrel and took Gray with him.

"Anything?"

"No more broadcasting bugs. How the hell did it get here? Who's goin' to know what else is hooked in here? I mean, we could be on Channel 13 right now."

"Enough. Did you check the bug for output?" Blue wasn't an electronics expert. But he had more than a smattering of the methodology and jargon.

"Right. 'Bout two milliwatts output, with a zero-gain antenna on the field-strength meter. The frequency is at the bottom of the FM band."

"So?"

"So, maybe a hundred-foot lateral effective area. Maybe twenty feet through the floor or ceiling. I figure there's a cheapo Sony receiver somewhere within the 38,000 cubic feet of space I'm talkin' 'bout. . . ."

"Cut that down-home shit, huh?"

"Don' y'all git uppity now, boss." He went really deep.

"Look . . ." Blue started. Then he decided to ignore the constant source of irritation in favor of getting on with it. "Uh, just get on with it."

"Anyways, that receiver probably has its audio wired into a recorder with a sound-actuated start."

Blue was chafing. He knew Gray was putting him on. It had been a long day and the "wired" that came out "wide" and the "recorder" that came out "recoder" grated on him. He endured. "So how do we proceed?" He could see that Gray was really warming to it. He would have loved to place a finger in Gray's eye.

"Oh. Well, we could rip the place apart, then start on the other floors. . . ."

Blue continued to endure. "Or?"

"Or we could try to get a high-gain antenna for the field-strength meter. If that little Jap transitor receiver box is like I think, maybe a little walkin' around could pick up a leak from the I.F. oscillator. Maybe save us a lot of tearin' 'round, 'cause maybe the bad guys have already removed the evidence of their transgressions."

"You do that. I'm going to check out Talon's home. I'll call in on the line in our workroom."

"Okay, boss."

29

Blue grumbled to himself about Gray's incessant drawl for the whole cab ride to 48 West Seventy-fifth Street. Eleven months of it. Enough is enough; he had to get a new partner. The spillover from that southern dip must be all over his own personnel-rating sheet. "Shit," he said, loud and with anguish.

"You got problems, sonny?" the short cabby asked, turning in the seat to view Blue like a fish through the plexiglass shield, ignoring the traffic. The heavy Yiddish tint to the driver's voice was the perfect counterpoint to Gray's cotton mouth.

"No. Don't you want to watch where you're going?"

"Mister with the bad mouth, I've been driving a taxi for thirty-two years. When advice I need, I'll ask. And you can't read signs?"

"Huh?"

"The smoking, mister. You can't see the sign?"

Blue focused in on the cab. All over, there were no-smoking signs, in English, French, Spanish, and who knows what other languages. There were characters that could have been Japanese or Chinese, maybe both. He stubbed out his cigarette and got madder at Gray. And at that creep Talon. New York. Jesus Christ, how he hated the place.

He gave the driver a dollar tip on the four-dollar fare and got out of the cab. He was thinking about his approach to the neighbors.

"They all do that."

"What?" He turned back to the driver, who was leaning out the window, speaking misty words in the brisk evening air.

"They all do that."

"No. I mean, what do they do?" He noticed something squishy underfoot and shuffled his right shoe.

"Big tips. It's the guilt. I can always tell someone with big guilt. First they smoke, then I say no, then it's a big tip. It always happens. Guilt. Watch your language, too." He rolled up the window and drove away.

Blue shuddered with frustration. He looked at the hundred-year-old brownstone and tried to set aside the boiling in his guts. There were steps going down to the entrance about five feet below the sidewalk. The second floor was just above eye level. He glanced around unconsciously, feeling a twinge between his shoulder blades after noticing members of various minority groups congregated in the area.

He walked to the steps. He scraped his right foot on the top one to remove the dog droppings he had squashed. They were all over the sidewalk. He opened the street door. Inside there was a hall with a locked security door. He searched the bell register and found Talon's name. He pressed the button. No response. He pressed the janitor's button.

"Hello?" a voice shouted from the small speaker.

He shouted back, "Janitor?"

"Who did you expect on my button, Onassis?"

Christ, they're all like this. New York. "I would like to talk with you."

"Speak up; I can't hear you!" The sound filled the tiny vestibule.

"I would like to talk with you."

"Better. No vacancies. See the agent."

He heard a click as the janitor hung up. He rang again.

"Hello?"

102

"I want to talk with you. Government business."

"I didn't hear the end of that."

Blue looked over his shoulder. "Government business," he said loudly.

"What government? Wait. I'll be right up."

Up from where? Blue thought he was on the bottom. In a few minutes a dirty face with a week-old beard looked cautiously out of the door.

"So?"

"May I come in?" Blue felt uncomfortable in the hallway.

"You got . . ."

"Here." Blue flashed Secret Service credentials. For internal use only.

"Come."

Blue followed the man down the hall. And down a long flight of stairs to the subbasement. Dust from the original coal-fired boiler, long since converted to oil, still floated there, lazy motes in the stifling, still air. Blue gagged, wanting to rip his clothes off and take a shower. The coal bin had been converted to a nine-by-twelve rat's nest.

"Sit."

The man was blotched from the leftover coal and had on what is now called a tank top, but was once known as an undershirt. He was short, old and so barrel-chested that his gut protruded in rolls between the undershirt bottom and pants top. He wore a pair of Penney's imitation Adidas sneakers which, where they were not dirty-blue-striped, were just dirty, to match the rest of the outfit. He also smelled ripe in the close air.

I'd love to have him in to fix my drain, thought Blue. "Cozy," he said, while stripping off his overcoat and jacket. He sat in a big chair with the stuffing erupting from it.

"I try," said the janitor.

Blue took out his notebook. "I'm making some inquiries about Mr. Joseph Talon. Can I have your name?"

"It's Pieter. P-I-E-T-E-R. Wynowski. W-Y-N-O-W-S-K-I. I'm the building engineer."

"Um. Been here long?"

"Yes."

"How long?"

"Maybe nine years."

"Do you know Mr. Talon?"

"Second-floor front. Sure. He comes in sometimes with these barfly bimbos. Wish I was thirty again, know what I mean?" He screwed up his face a bit.

Blue had seen the beaver-shot cutouts the walls were well on their way to being completely covered with. He knew exactly what Wynowski meant. "Sure."

"But he's got this new one now. A real piece of resistance. Know what I mean? Covered up a lot. An ass that you want to bite, but it's so fast goin' by you'd only catch a tooth on the pants. Know what I mean?"

"Sure. Got her name?"

"Nah. They come; they go. Mostly come." Chuckle. "Know what I mean?"

Blue was suffocating. The air had to weigh forty pounds a chestful. "Sure. How about any others?"

"Nope. Sorry."

"Seen him lately?"

The man looked a bit uncomfortable. "What's he done?" He was fishing for some gossip.

"This is a routine check."

"That's what the other guys said, too. 'Routine.' It must be something. Right?"

"Other guys?" Blue looked uncomfortable.

"Sure. Saturday afternoon. More cops."

"Cops?"

"Something. Like you. No names, a quick flash of those free-lunch-and-subway plastic cards. All questions, no answers."

"You don't know where they were from?"

"Do I know where you're from? Know what I mean?"

"Um. What did they look like?"

"Don't you guys work together? They looked like you. About six feet of white cop."

"What did you tell them?" Blue was getting very nervous.

"Same thing I'm telling you. Know what I mean? Ask a question. I'll tell you."

"Sure. Sure. Well, I guess that's it."

"You don't want to look at the scene of the crime?"

"You let them in?"

"Sure." He held out his hand.

Blue took it and started shaking hands. Mr. Wynowski looked indignant.

"No. Not to shake." He pulled his hand away from Blue's firm grasp. "Cross it; don't shake it."

Blue had only twelve dollars left from his travel-expense money. He pulled it out of his pocket and handed it over. Wynowski looked hurt.

"Twelve bucks?"

"All I've got." Blue had about eighty cents in change and a healthy distaste for New York subways.

"They gave me fifty." He wasn't moving.

"That's it." Nothing happened. Blue emptied his pants pocket. "I've got eighty cents in change for the subway."

The janitor simultaneously grabbed the change and reached into his pants. He pulled out a token. "Eighty cents is eighty cents."

"I need a dime for a call. In case." Blue took the token.

The janitor grudgingly handed him back a dime. "Well, let's go."

"When's the last time you saw him?"

"Talon?"

"Yeah." Blue was gathering up the clothing he had taken off.

"Around Friday. But I heard him on Saturday."

"Doing what?"

"Starting his sickle."

"Sickle?"

"Motorsickle."

"Where?"

"In the street."

"When?"

"Maybe around noon. At least, I think it was him. See, I had the chute open. For ventilation." He pointed up to a rectangular black hole in the top of the wall. "Where they used to deliver the coal. Anyway, I heard this sickle start, and when I went to check the garbage cans later, it was gone."

"From where?"

"He had it chained to the no-parking sign out in front."

"Oh. Did you tell those other guys?"

"Sure. For fifty bucks, would I hold out? Know what I mean?"

"Yeah. Tell them anything else?" Blue was getting really sick to his stomach.

"No. But they were interested in the tire."

"What tire?"

"That one." The janitor pointed, and Blue focused on a corner heaped with a pile of odds and ends.

He stepped over and looked at it. "Why?"

"Who knows? I told them Mr. Talon threw it out last Thursday. They wanted to take it with them. But they wouldn't give me another ten for it."

"Can I have it?" Who knew what it meant? Better be safe.

"The belt?"

Wynowski eyed Blue's brass imitation Wells-Fargo presentation buckle.

"Okay."

30

They went up to Talon's apartment. Blue held his coat and jacket over his arm and held up his pants with that hand. He carried the tire in the other. He noticed that his shirt looked as though he'd been downwind from a smudge pot. The air at the first-floor hallway was a spring breeze, diminished somewhat by Mr. Wynowski, who was leading the way.

"Don't be too long."

"I won't."

"Don't forget the tire."

"No, I won't."

"And don't steal anything."

"No." Blue was too overwhelmed to be indignant.

"I mean, cops are like that. Know what I mean?"

"Sure."

The last phase of unlocking the door over, Wynowski stepped aside to let Blue in.

"So long," the janitor said.

At least he left off the "sucker," thought Blue. "So long."

He closed the door behind him and cut off the waves of B.O. He dropped the tire, coat and jacket, and let his pants sag. The phone was right there. He dialed Gray.

"Hello."

"Hello. I'm in Talon's apartment."

"Is it bugged?"

"Uh, no. I've checked around as much as possible. But maybe we should sweep it." Blue dragged the phone to the kitchen and turned on the water in the sink. Brilliant. He wanted to shoot the drawling son of a bitch.

"Well, I found the recorder," Gray said. The honeysuckle in his voice was not so prominent after his success with the field-strength meter.

"Fine. I'll talk to you about that later. . . ."

"You're *in* the apartment?"

"Right, I . . ."

"Shit. What about clearance? Remember that creep Ellsberg? I don't want my ass in a sling, man."

"I wasn't the first in here, Bo. Someone else is sniffing around our bird. No time." That southern fucker. Always trying to get him off guard. "Anyway, our bird had a motorcycle. Get hold of M.V.B. and try to run it down." Blue was triumphant.

"Shit, man, I got one or two lil' things hea' myself." Down home.

Blue clenched his teeth, while Gray warmed up.

"Anyways, Ah checked the New York po-lice department, stahtin' in Manhattan aftah Ah found the recordin' stuff. Ah found a interestin' accident when Ah got to Queens."

Cut the damn preamble, redneck. "Yes?"

"On Sunday evenin', 'bout eleven, there was an accident in Jackson Heights. A car and a motorcycle. The latter vehicle was registered in the name of Joseph Talon."

Blue tugged at his pants. He wanted to strangle him. "Our bird?"

"Don't know. There were two charcoaled people, both male. The car and motorcycle were burned up, too."

"See if we can make a dental I.D. Get everything you can from the city cops." Shit.

"Yowser."

Blue hung up. He took a swipe at his forehead with a clenched fist. Then he started a systematic search and came up with a systematic nothing. Especially no little black book.

Ladies' clothes were hung up in a broom closet, and there were some more in a big suitcase, but nothing else. Not even a name.

He thumbed through the Manhattan phone directory and saw a few pencil marks, so he wadded his coat around the book. He kicked the tire, then decided to try to get his belt back. He went back downstairs. Wynowski was adamant. Blue chucked the tire into the gutter outside. Then he caught the subway downtown, holding his pants up.

Something funny was going on. The accident had happened on Saturday night. The two others who'd been through Talon's apartment earlier certainly hadn't been there to check on Talon's next of kin. But since they hadn't been back after the accident, they had probably gotten what . . .

He didn't know that they hadn't been back. Or that they weren't back at that moment, watching or listening from someplace. He made a note in his book. Better stake the place out.

Blue tried to focus on the facts. Shit, he thought, if it wasn't for that down-home asshole crimping his style, he could think better.

31

Talon awoke, finally, with his sorrow. He had fought to remain asleep. Roxanne Plotnik's ultramodern apartment, with the carpet that looked like it needed a haircut, was dark. He ached with his loss and his pain. Worst of all, he couldn't say why these things had happened. When something awful is happening, it should have a source. Some identifiable genesis a rational person can recognize and either change or live with. He had no such point of reference for the pyre that had burned up a part of his life only twenty hours before.

He had walked the Hell Gate. In more than one idiom he had trod that dangerous trail. He had vague recollections of the long climb down from the trestle on emergency stairs to Ward's Island, then across the Harlem River on a footbridge to 103rd Street in upper Manhattan. He had then walked downtown.

In Yorkville he'd found a bar and spent fifteen minutes in the men's room, cleaning dried blood from his head and hair. The stains on his jacket were permanent. His ears were still ringing and oozing watery blood.

Then he got a drink and Roxanne Plotnik had appeared, a queen on a bar stool. A Jewish Sister of Mercy. A shower and a couch. Fifteen hours of fitful sleep. Now darkness and sadness.

He felt like vomiting, but nothing came of it. It was seven-thirty in the evening. Miss Plotnik had not returned from work or whatever drinking establishment she frequented Mondays. He felt empty, and anxiety twisted up his gut. He sat in the dark and tried to get a handle on things.

He got up and took a shower, shaved, and dressed in the pants and turtleneck he'd worn Saturday, when Carlee was his soul's desire and alive.

He wanted to do something, call someone, go somewhere. But inevitably there was nothing, no one, nowhere. He had never felt so empty. Alone. The Aikido regimen didn't help. He meditated for half an hour, the sonorous mantra droning in his mind. No help. No succor.

Eight-thirty. Still dark, still nowhere. A key turned in the lock. The lights came on.

"You're still here."

"Right."

"I might have had company, plans." Factual, no hint of annoyance.

"I would have left unobtrusively."

She hustled into the kitchen with a couple of Gristede's bags clutched in front of her.

"I'll make you something to eat. What would you like?"

"What do you have?"

"Breakfasty stuff?"

"Sounds fine."

"Eggs, toast, marmalade, pickled herring, beer?"

"Leave out the herring, and it's fine." He hadn't moved.

"You look like you got mugged by the Creature from the Black Lagoon. Walking in Central Park?" She stood in front of him, holding a tall frosty beer glass full of Piel's. "It's not great beer, but it's cold."

"Thanks."

"Any port in a storm." She gave a high-pitched sarcastic laugh.

A neurotic thirty-five-year-old Florence Nightingale, he thought. "Right."

"You didn't have to agree with me." She looked at him from the kitchen entrance.

Not bad. Better than most of the Bronx beauties. "No, I'll leave."

"Please don't. I don't want to be alone. Stay. I'll be good. Promise."

I really need this, he thought. But he did. "Okay."

"What's your name?"

"Joe."

"Joe what? You wouldn't tell me last night."

"Joe's okay."

"Are you in trouble?"

"I'm still breathing. No."

"No, are you in trouble?"

"Yes."

"What?"

"I don't know."

"I'm hard-boiling the eggs. I'd better get them. Wait a minute."

She came out with the food on a tray.

"Salt?" he said.

"It's not good for you. I don't have it," she said.

"A hard-boiled egg without salt is inedible."

"I'll borrow from next door."

"In New York? There's probably a flasher waiting for you with his teenie weenie. Forget it."

"What kind of trouble?"

"I still don't know."

"Did you do something bad?"

"Not that I can remember."

"I mean, you don't get violent or anything?"

"Only when I can't get salt."

"Oh."

"Right."

"What's wrong with you?" she said.

"I think it's a concussion, maybe some cracked ribs. Nothing serious."

"You lie like a rug."

"That's old."

"I'm only twenty-eight."

He wanted to see the driver's license. "I'll stay."

"You're invited."

"Right. All I need is an armful of morphine and a bunch of tape for my chest. The ribs."

"Darvon?"

"Right."

"I've got some."

"And some wetting solution for my eyes. I haven't had my contact lenses out for two days."

112

"I'll go to the corner drugstore."

"I'll pay."

"Of course."

An hour later, he still had a blood-tinged discharge from his right ear and some sticking inside his back. But most of the pain was submerged in the effect of the little pink and gray pills. He needed a navigation aid to cross the living room sea. The carpet had white caps, and he felt giddy. The last thing he remembered that Monday night was leaving his contacts exposed to the vagaries of the atmosphere on a bathroom shelf and Miss Plotkin saying, "Why don't we lie down." It really was no question.

32

He woke up for real a little after six Tuesday morning. She was snoring next to him. He had a hazy recollection of raiding the Darvon and Excedrin during the night. The pillow he had been resting his head on was wet with sweat and the discharge from his ear. Maybe some tears, too.

He gathered his possessions together. He cleaned up. He scribbled an incoherent note of thanks on a handy pad of engraved Jensen note paper, set it next to Miss Plotkin's authentic Cartier tank watch and took off. The doorman looked at him with one eye while the other continued sleeping.

Talon saw that he was on Seventy-ninth between First and York. He'd been hibernating in a fancy high-rise. Now he set off with a lingering dizziness. One block west, he caught a Second Avenue bus downtown. He got off at Forty-third

Street, walked to Forty-second, and then went west again to Bryant Park. He picked a bench and sat in the marginal morning grayness, waiting for his mind to clear. It didn't.

He left his bench, found a Chock Full o' Nuts, and endured the wait, one of the hundreds of customers breathing down the necks of persons already seated and gulping down coffee and donuts. Likewise Talon. He gulped and chewed and felt the energy of those behind him forcing him to eat and drink even faster, to the point where he took one of his donuts with him and fled for the door.

The Darvon and the problems it was masking were combining to take Talon on a trip. It was just by dint of good fortune and the host of other nodding, dazed and ragged citizens in Bryant Park that he was not arrested. He would have been a prime candidate for the meat wagon in a lot of places.

He surveyed his options. He could not go home. He could not go to the office. Home, his carrel, and the subway had been ninety percent of his life's elapsed time for years. The other ten percent was bars where he picked up the occasional chick to take home. It was too early for the bars, and he had nowhere to go on the subway. He was stymied.

He could call the office, but he couldn't think of anything to say or who to say it to. He could go to the Hilton and collect his gear cache, but he couldn't think of anywhere to go or what to do with it. So he levered himself off the bench and got a *New York Times*.

Back at the bench, he turned to the crossword puzzle. He dug around in his bag and found a pen. By nine-thirty he was short six or seven words, cold, and ready for another of Miss Plotkin's magic pills. Figuring on at least solving his creature comfort problem, he gathered his gear and headed for the grande dame of midtown, the main branch of the New York Public Library.

33

"You want to check that?" the black guard asked, looking very toothy and well scrubbed. He didn't have a moustache, which was unusual.

"No, I thought I'd take it in with me." The canvas bag was his sole possession, except the clothes he wore.

"We'll search it on the way out. It's up to you."

"*Honi soit qui mal y pense,*" said Talon.

"But only in this rash, insane and importunate world of ours," said the guard. "*Ceteris paribus, cave canem.*"

"Huh?" said Talon.

"Just meeting grandiloquence with grandiloquence. All things being equal, beware of the dog. Somewhat more apt than your Order of the Garter swipe . . ."

"Evil to him who evil thinks of it," volunteered Talon. He was hopeful that the bombast he had unleashed might be short-circuited. He didn't think his head could survive it.

"Quite so," said the guard. "However, it was not a question of *j'accuse,* but one of convenience for the visiting public. Being searched is not pleasant, and for a man of your *visage et condition* it might be a bit more emphatic. . . ."

"Enthusiastic?"

"Yes, better."

"See ya."

"Doubtless, *si tu pense.*"

"Right."

Talon settled himself down in the main reading room on the third floor. He started to contemplate the Sanroc debacle.

Somebody out there didn't like him. There was a mutuality in that feeling. His mind wandered to surfing at the ranch and then came back. Someone had killed Carlee and tried to kill him. He mused over Annabel Lee for a few moments, seeing Carlee shut up in a sepulcher. Winged seraphs came and took her away.

His mind snapped back. The pain was coming back, and he jiggled the handful of Darvon capsules in his pocket. But he couldn't think straight with them in his brain, so he decided to wait. He finally decided that he wanted three things. A solution of the mystery for his intellect, protection for his very mortal physical being, and revenge to satisfy his soul.

His mind wandered again into a non-Aikido series of fantasies involving excruciating pain and slow death for whoever had killed Carlee. Their karma indicated that the fantasies would happen in truth. But karma would take time, and time . . .

Talon came back to reality, and then he started a deep meditation, the mantra taking the place of his mental meanderings.

He felt refreshed twenty minutes later. He kept the mind slippage to a minimum and concentrated on the facts. Somewhere he had stepped on some big toes. But whose? It could be at the Company, at the N.R.O., or somewhere else; it might not even be related to the square cloud, although he thought it had to be. Whoever the toes belonged to, Talon was a man alone. No one could help. On top of everything else, he'd killed one, maybe two men. It didn't look good.

Waves of anxiety hit him, compounded by the terrible loneliness he felt. He started to wander again before he came back to reality, or to the closest approximation of it he could manage.

There was only one way for the square cloud to have gotten to his desk, as a substitution for the image Sanroc had

116

trapped with its ubiquitous eye and normally broadcast back to earth by telemetry. It had to be, in light of the unrealistic reference material he had gotten for quadrant R201 from the computer.

It had to be substitution during telemetry. That way the image would always be a cloud. And when the image was compared by the computer with the phony reference-material norm, there would never be an aberration.

How could it be done? He had no clue about the electronic intricacies of Sanroc. Maybe he could find someone who did.

He wandered down to the Science and Technology room, on the first floor. He pulled the biographical reference drawer. He had some trouble trying to decide where he was going. Then he picked up on the title *Men of Space*. He gathered up his canvas bag and the *Times* and headed for the stacks.

Finding the book was easy. It even had pictures of the vaunted space pioneers of the early sixties. Trying to figure out which genius could give him the information he needed was a whole new problem. Space optics, computers and telemetry were the areas to look for. He could forget the hardware men.

And then, simply, he found the man he thought could answer the questions. Helmut Ehrenzweig.

Ehrenzweig had more degrees than a thermometer. Fifty-six years old when the book was published, older than Von Braun, and out of the limelight, he was one of many scientists liberated from Nazi Germany who had become United States citizens and mainstays of the space effort. He had been the ground-guidance and ballistic director in the development of the V-2 and Wasserfall at Peenemünde on the Baltic from 1938 to the bitter end in '45.

No slouch after the war, he had accumulated mastery in the fields of laser technology, radar, radio, and optical earth scans and data transmission. In the early sixties, he'd been based in Huntsville, Alabama, with the Redstone Arsenal Missile Development Division. The photo showed strong, committed eyes, a large nose, and a full moustache over a smile. Talon quietly removed the page from the book. The picture could be helpful.

Talon warmed up. His mind wasn't clearing, but he was concentrating a bit better. He wanted another pill for the pain, but he waited.

He located the *New York Times Index* and checked the years from 1963 on. No obituary on Ehrenzweig. A small article referenced in 1975 about a speech in Munich to the *Gessellschaft für Raketentechnik und Raumfahrt* on data recovery from fly-by surveys of Mars. Better and better. He was probably still alive.

Who's Who in America failed to show biographical information on the man. But it did show his son Paul, an executive with Allied Chemical who was degreed to the hilt, just like Papa. Not the least were an M.B.A. from Harvard and a Ph.D. from Stanford. Lots of other letters. Paul's home was in Summit, New Jersey.

Talon folded his tent and went back to the main reading room. He sat down again with his *Times* crossword and got one word in fifteen minutes. He leafed through the paper and found himself staring at a picture of Joseph Talon on page seven. There it was. The rather foggy story was about a double vehicular homicide and Talon being wanted in connection therewith. A complete description followed. The reporter had to have talked with someone who had seen Talon recently. The description had his eye color as brown.

In Philadelphia, nearly everyone reads the *Enquirer*. In New York, it's the *Times*. Now Sulzberger's out to get me, Talon thought. Shit. He felt as though he were on *Candid Camera*, with everyone watching.

He looked up over the sea of blue lampshades. Sure enough, the black Teddy Nadler, guardian of the portals, was leading a parade into the room. Second in line was a shortish, stoutish woman with subhuman features, wearing a dashiki. Third and fourth were a pair of New York's finest. The woman was eighty feet away from Talon and pointing her informer's finger right at him.

Talon popped out his brown contacts, dropped them into his canvas bag along with his wallet, and booted the bag across the aisle. He wrinkled up his features and put his aching head down on the table.

A few seconds later, he felt the inevitable tap on his shoulder and heard the woman assuring John Law that Talon was their man.

He had no trouble affecting a bleary, myopic stare.

"Yes?"

"Pardon me, sir, but this lady has called us to the library."

Sir again. He shivered. "My name is Arthur Parks, officer. What's this all about?"

"Do you have some identification, sir?"

"Well, uh, no. I'm afraid that I was the victim of carelessness and left my wallet at home." He reached to the *Times* and closed it. "I'm sure there must be a mistake." He refrained from declaiming his innocence to the watching throng. But the rattle of handcuffs was loud in his ears.

"I know he's the man. I saw him."

"This lady claims . . ."

"There must be a mistake. I've got blue eyes," Talon said.

The cop looked puzzled. "Look, sir. I can see you got blue eyes. We get complaints here all the time. Mostly weenie-wavers and fruits. This is different, understand? She says she saw you ripping up a book. So?"

"Uh. Right. No one with blue eyes and a hangover would destroy library property." Thin.

"I saw him ripping up a book. Tearing it to shreds." She was a litle glassy-eyed and very loud. "It was in Sci- and Tech-biographical."

"Nonsense," said Talon. "Ask her what book." He looked fatigued, nearsighted and righteously indignant. Never trust a righteous man, woman or child. Especially the latter two. And as for the first, look at George McGovern. Talon thought about it and waited.

"I'm . . . I'm not sure which book. He was just tearing it up." Resignation.

"What did I do with it? Eat it?"

"I'm not sure." Defeat.

"Thank you all for ruining my morning." Talon picked up the *Times* and waited.

"Sorry, *sir*." The cop didn't sound it.

"It's your job." Magnanimous.

The lady was weeping with frustration as the cops led her away.

"Smooth move, Charlie."

"Right," said Talon.

The erudite guard leaned over the table. "This is my home. Home sweet home."

"James McNeill Whistler."

"His mother, mutha'. I don't want no shit on my doorstep, dig? So I'm givin' you jus' five minutes to fly, Charlie. Dig? Or I'm goin' to take you by the stacks an' lay the *Iliad* up side yo' head. I don't like no action I don't understand. So you fly, brown eyes, 'fo' I add black to the blue."

"Right." Talon got up and almost fainted. He collected his canvas bag and split. He was shaking a lot.

120

34

Talon found a phone booth and got the number for Paul Ehrenzweig in Summit. Then he made a person-to-person call to Dr. Helmut Ehrenzweig. He listened while a female voice explained to the operator that the senior Ehrenzweig was out of town and would not be home until six-thirty that evening.

Talon went to the Kentucky Fried Chicken outlet where Grant's used to be. He went to the bathroom and put his contacts back in. He gagged down some greasy nondescript pieces of pressure-cooked chicken and a Pepsi. Then he bought his way into a Forty-second Street triple-feature theater headlining Blacula and two Jimmy Brown dogs. He slept for two hours, both arms hugging his worldly possessions.

He woke up at three, walked out, and found an Army-Navy store, where he purchased a pea jacket, a wool cap, faded Lee denims, a shirt, and a black boatneck sweater. He bought a duffel bag and threw in his old clothes and his canvas carry-all.

He looked at himself in a mirror. With the wool cap pulled down and the jacket collar up, he looked just like what he was: a guy on the run wearing a brand-new camouflage suit.

He took the subway down to Wall Street and huddled in the graveyard at Trinity Church until a little after four that afternoon, when the exodus from Manhattan started. He joined the increasing number of people headed for the World Trade Center and took the PATH subway to Hackensack.

There he caught the venerable Erie-Lackawanna for Summit. He arrived at the Summit station at five-fifteen.

The depot was closed. He waited and got very cold. His only respite came when he ran to check the passengers from each arriving train, east or westbound, for the rocket genius.

35

"Somethin' funny's going on here," Gray announced that Tuesday morning at nine-thirty, as Blue and Miss D'Arcy stepped into the work cubicle.

"I agree," said Blue. He wasn't sure what he was agreeing with. He had endured a fitful night's sleep at the Shelbourne Hotel, a midtown C-class operation catering to traveling salespersons, Shriners, visiting rock musicians and sub–GS-16 government types. Gray had a separate but equal room. While shaving his face baby-bottom smooth that morning, Blue had made up his mind to avoid taking umbrage at Gray's affectations. He felt ragged and drained. It might have been the eight-martini nightcap. He looked at Gray's enthusiastic face, rolled-up sleeves, and neat piles of paper, and started to bridle.

Gray hadn't said anything else but had continued to stare at Miss D'Arcy until she got the message and left. "First and fo'most is the bug. The only one in the place, and it's in Talon's office. Why a place where there's no meetings? It's just a carrel."

"To relay messages to confederates?"

"Not if you hear the tape we got. A bunch of mumbles

122

and . . . Anyway, I've got some people at the home office working on it."

"Oh." Blue was shaking off his morning malaise and feeling better now that Gray had forgotten his deep-South honey-pot act. Blue was a little confused. He did not like to lose control. "I suppose it was to check on what he was doing?"

"I suppose so. But what was he doing that forty-four other C.P.R. readers weren't?"

"I guess we'd better find out." Brilliant.

"Um, yes."

"What else?" said Blue.

"The receiver-recorder. It was on top of the swing arm of a fire hose in a cabinet at the end of this hallway. Right next to an emergency exit."

"So anyone in this operation could have placed and serviced the recorder."

"Plus the janitorial staff."

"They're all security-cleared."

"So's everyone else in this place." Zap.

"Yes," said Blue.

"It seems unlikely that we'd have more than one intruder, correct?"

"Unlikely, yes."

"So the field is narrowed down."

"To the janitorial staff and everyone else. That's narrow?"

"No. Just the two on the cleanup, plus Flynn and D'Arcy," said Gray.

"Why?"

"The locks on the carrels. They're Medoc high-security. The special key can't be duplicated. Only the cleanup people have a passkey. You remember Flynn's got one for each carrel locked up in his office. But he and D'Arcy have to open up a double safe-deposit lock, each using his or her own key, which . . ."

"Can be duplicated."

"You guessed 'er, Chester. Also, there have been only two janitors sweeping the carrels in this place in the last year. The battery in the bug is good for only about four months, and it's still hot."

I'll get this smart redneck, Blue thought. "Okay, so we've got some closets to check. We'd better . . ."

"I've got a couple of people working on it. From the home office."

"Of course." Jesus, when had this drawling dip got all this done?

Gray picked up a pad. "Talon had the habit of ordering a bunch of extra C.P.R.s . . ."

Blue looked up.

"Computer Photo Remakes. From Sanroc. That's what he was working on."

Blue was uncomfortable. He wasn't that familiar with the jargon. "Of course."

"Well, he ordered lots of extras. Over a long period of time. Lots of different areas. Talon told Flynn that the reason was to check the beaches for 'surf and tits.' That's a direct quote. That's why the big stock of C.P.R.s."

"Anything there?"

"We'll check through it, but I eyeballed some of them through the magnifying glass. Sure enough, there were tits and surf. Next, we've got the accident.

"All the police would tell us," Gray continued, "was that Talon's motorcycle cracked up and burned. Fifty feet away was a 1975 Ford Granada, also burned up. Inside were two male Caucasians, well-done, no identifying documents. Hertz car. Phony address. The passenger was dead prior to the fire, by virtue of a crushed windpipe. Someone made sauce out of his Adam's apple."

"Talon? Did they check dentals?"

"Well," Gray drawled, "as a sort of eliminator, I asked for

124

blood types. Neither matched Talon's, according to the information Miss Shiffler got from Palo Alto."

"Good. Fine. So we've got two John Does and no Talon."

"Kee-rect! Incidentally, I arranged a surveillance on his apartment, just in case. Now for the rest of the information. Did you read the *Times* this morning?"

Where did the bastard get the hours to do all this stuff? "Not yet."

"Look at this." Gray showed him the clipping.

Blue looked at Talon's photo. "Jesus, the cops are really on the ball. This should help."

"Well," Gray drew it out, "maybe not. There's two things I see that don't compute. The photo and the description."

"How's that?" Blue quickly scanned the article again. Nothing.

"The photo's the same as the one *we* got from the State Department . . . from his passport," said Gray. "State says they never gave a copy out."

"I thought it might have been from the Motor Vehicle Bureau—you know, for his license," Blue said.

"They only do that for chauffeur's licenses in New York."

"Oh . . . maybe the cops who searched Talon's place got it from his passport." Flat.

"Which cops?"

"The janitor said he let in two plainclothesmen."

Gray made a note in his book. "Find out anything?"

Blue thought about his belt. Who the hell was running this thing? "Nothing. Just about the motorcycle and some unnamed woman who's been living with Talon for the last week or so. She wasn't around."

"No address books?"

"Just the Manhattan directory, with some marks. I'm checking it out." He'd forgotten it at the Shelbourne. Shit.

Another note and Gray said, "Anyways, the description. You notice?"

"Huh?"

"It's got brown eyes."

"So?"

"The license bureau says blue. I checked with Flynn. Talon wears contacts. Brown contacts over blue irises. So, brown eyes. Flynn says for about six months."

"Why?"

"Who knows? He's some ex-surfer type, minor genius. Like the C.P.R.s he ordered. Who knows?"

"What's it matter? Either it was a goof by the police, or . . ."

"They had to get their information from the M.V.B. . . . *if* the story came from the police. . . .

"But let me tell you this," Gray went on. "One, with all the crime in this city, it seems a little out of character to print a story, description and photo of this guy. I don't know that they would do that today for John Dillinger. Two, both the cops and the editor I talked to at the *Times* were evasive as hell when I asked them about the story. At least the editor owned up to the fact that the story was printed as received—brown eyes."

Gray was really doing his homework.

"Finally, the *News* and the *Post* both have identical stories, no source available."

"Oh."

Gray looked as if he were ready to sniff the breeze for a scent. "Something is going on."

"No doubt," said Blue.

"What?"

"Who knows?"

"Someone in this goddamn office knows," said Gray.

"Brown eyes, passport photo, and bug."

"Seems to go in the same direction."

"Seems that way." Blue wished he hadn't had those martinis at The Cattleman. But damn, those ladies looked good. He wished he could have afforded one. The goddamn

Shelbourne again tonight. And only one shirt. He'd have to do some washing in the sink. He wondered whether Gray had scrounged up some more expense money.

". . . to Octopus," Gray finished.

"What?"

"The only long-distance call Talon made in the last two months was for an hour and a half on Saturday—to Octopus. I got a print-out from Ma Bell. It was on your list. You look a little tired today." Gray gave him a knowing look. "He called from his home. As far as we know, the call ended at Octopus, but there's no time-base record. No tape to show the Saturday use."

"No record?" He had no idea what a time-base record was. This guy was driving him crazy.

"Kee-rect. Without the log-in, we have no idea what he was doing or what program was addressed. Either the guy's brilliant and figured a shunt around the time-base-recording system, or we had a malfunction."

"This thing is really turning into a bucket of worms."

"Or, there's another alternative."

"Huh?"

"Someone at Langley could have fixed the time-base tape."

"At Octopus?"

"Maybe. That's two people, not counting the turkeys that got cooked. One here, one down there."

"Seems a bit far-fetched. I mean, what you're talking is some kind of conspiracy thing in the Company. With Talon fitting in as either an apostate, a dupe or a target."

"Just so."

"In the Company?"

"Doubtful, ace, but somewhere."

"He's in serious trouble, then."

"If he's even still alive. Don't you want to know how he contacted Octopus?"

The fucker's going to get me again. "How do you mean?"

"Well, you don't just phone up and say 'how y'all?' to Octopus."

"Sure, you have to have the access numbers and program calls. But there's nothing any of these clerk types can get that any citizen couldn't find by going to the library."

"And spend ten years finding. No, to get access to Octopus you need a computer terminal."

"Oh. Yes."

"A portable telex-computer terminal was removed from an Ag Department office on this floor last week."

"Talon."

"Seems like. Did you see anything looking like one of those things in his place?"

"No." Blue was certain he'd have spotted it.

"Then he's got it."

"How, on a motorcycle?"

"Maybe he stashed it somewhere." The accent was really toned down now.

"I wonder whether we can try a trace if he calls into Langley again," said Blue. Oh, how intelligent.

"I've got some people working on that."

"Sure." Prick. "I'm going to get his phone book checked. Right after I check out the pile of aerial photos, the C.P.R.s. By the way, did you get any more expense money?"

"Yeah," Gray said. He looked disgusted.

Blue pulled the hand truck with the C.P.R.s into Talon's carrel. After nine hours of bleary-eyed looking, he had seen a lot of waves, beaches and bodies. He had dismissed the cloud-cover photo out of hand. It was an easy decision because, after all, there wasn't anything to see. He went back to his hotel at eight-thirty that night to pick up the directory and a belt. In the bar.

36

About that time, Talon was still stomping around the Summit station. His aches had been aggravated by the cold weather. And the cheap surplus-store clothes didn't work that well. He checked the photo of Ehrenzweig for the umpteenth time.

Either Talon had missed him, or he wasn't coming by rail.

An eastbound train pulled in. Talon decided to take it back to the city. Since he was on the westbound side, he ran downstairs and through the underpass which he had been using for passage all evening. His head was bothering him, and his ribs hurt. He was bumping through the commuter crowd when he spotted his man.

"Dr. Ehrenzweig!"

"Yes?"

Talon, out of breath and poised for a run up the stairs to the eastbound platform, couldn't get anything else out. The good scientist resembled the photo, with a few more crinkles.

"You look not so good."

Talon shook his head. The guy sounded like Artie Johnson.

"Well, what is it you want? I'm late for dinner."

Talon rested his hand on the banister. "Just a few minutes." Bela Lugosi, maybe.

"Well?" Ehrenzweig started to walk again.

Talon turned and walked with him, still trying to get some breath control. "Help."

"Are you in trouble?"

"I think so."

"We have ways of making you talk." Ehrenzweig glanced at Talon. His eyes were clear, sparkling.

Talon grinned. "I'm sure."

"Contact lenses?"

"Right."

"The description said blue eyes. I was prepared to be more guarded, you see. But I think you do not seem much a desperado. So, for the good of the new Fatherland and my old frail bones I will cooperate. Coffee?"

"Yes."

"It is good. You are very pale."

"Right."

Ehrenzweig led Talon from the station to a coffee shop. They sat and ordered. It was hot inside.

"Well, Mr. Talon. What can a man who cooks up his fellow human beings want with me?"

"You have an amazing memory." Talon sat in awe of the man.

"I think that is not what you want. You are on the run, and yet you have come to a stranger. I am no good for a hostage. I am not known to harbor wanted men. So I imagine you have a scientific question for me."

"Right."

"I prefer 'yes' or 'correct,' not directions."

"Yes." Talon wondered whether two prima donnas could mesh.

"I am privy to many security matters. These I would not reveal. My memory still serves me well in other matters. Like the story and photograph in the *Daily News*."

"*Times*."

"Then both papers must have had it. Interesting. There was a discarded *News* in the train, which I read. My morning's *Times* awaits my return home. So you require my help?"

"Right. Yes."

"And you offer?"

"Offer?"

"The *quid pro quo*, the consideration for the bargain. The coffee, while welcome and excellent, is insufficient. I trust you will do the honors?"

"Yes."

"Regardless, I exact payment, in dollars, marks, yen, or what have you. Or . . ."

"Or what?" Talon's pain pounded in his temples. This beautiful old gentleman, for all his acuity, was Deutsching him to death. Talon felt faint.

"Or something else of value."

"I have nothing of value. A little money."

"My years were bought dear, and, accordingly, my minutes now are sold dear. You see, a word, even, is as valuable to me now as a day of my youth."

Talon clawed at his sweater, pulled off the pea jacket, and continued to sweat. "That's it?"

"As you say, 'that's it.' For now."

"What does the last part mean?"

"The thing of value might be information."

"Huh?"

"'What?' is better."

"Yes. What information?"

"You may know something I don't. That will be apparent shortly. If so, the trade will be of adequate dimensions. So tell me about what it is that is happening to you."

"I'm not sure I know."

"The best you can."

"I must know whether you will tell anyone."

"I am not a priest. On the other hand, I'm not a politician

131

or a bureaucrat, either. You must leave it to my discretion. After all, *you* are looking for aid. However, you may gain some assurance from the fact that I have not yet called for police assistance."

"No. You haven't." Talon had heard the "yet" loud and clear.

"Please begin."

Talon looked around the grimy interior of the coffee shop, then back at the old man. Ehrenzweig's recall of the *News* article was amazing. The guy was getting him off balance. Taking control. Talon let it happen. What the hell? He began talking.

He rambled a lot. The old man had his eyes closed and might have been asleep. For twenty minutes Talon talked, and then Ehrenzweig's eyes snapped open.

"Tits and surf?"

"Yes, my lunch-hour life."

"Tits I know about. Surf, I do not. How much do you?"

"From the time I was eight I was out there waiting. The surf was my life for years."

"You have expertise?"

"Yes."

"One more question. Why brown eyes?"

"I got tired of looking at the same old face in the morning. Last year there was a moustache."

"Good. Now for the bargain. You will explain the surfing, and I will do my best to help you with nonsensitive information. A bargain?"

"Yes. I agree."

"Good. Then we shall leave and go to a restaurant to eat a fine meal, drink some Schnapps, and conclude our arrangement."

Talon managed a weak smile. He paid for the coffee and followed Ehrenzweig out the door. Like the Kaiser's guard, Talon thought. He walks like he'll live forever.

They went to the station parking lot. Talon waited while Ehrenzweig put his key in the lock of a vintage Mercedes as well groomed as its owner.

"My one extravagance of any magnitude."

It smelled only of leather. No cigarettes. Talon thought about how long it had been since he had smoked a Kool, and he got a thickness in the back of his throat. Later he'd get one. "It's beautiful."

"A 220 convertible. Nineteen sixty-one. My pride and joy."

Ehrenzweig drove smartly, shifting up and down, braking lightly, and turning precisely. After a few minutes, he parked at Rod's 1890 House.

Rod's is an experience. To start with, the place is a treat for the eyes. The dining room is set in a railroad passenger car, fitted out in true *fin de siècle* opulence. Talon felt out of place, but no one else seemed to mind. The maître d' welcomed "Herr Doctor" warmly.

The meal that followed was excellent. Both men had settled for Maine lobster, preceded by salmon *fumé* and a small green salad. Talon skipped most of the wine, but had one glass for taste. Throughout dinner, the subject was surfing. Talon did most of the talking.

They decided to skip dessert. During coffee, the old man asked a few questions.

"How long does it take to learn?"

"Quickly or slowly or never. I assume that by 'learn' you mean a reasonable degree of skill."

"Quite right. Quite right. You think I am too old?"

"You?"

"Of course, me. I ski each year at Innsbruck. I am no spring chicken, but the feathers are not yet plucked."

"You would have to go where the waves are good. Perfect. And learn right. Hawaii." Carlee. Later.

"You could teach me?"

"I could. If I'm alive."

"Good, then that is our next bargain. I will have to give you something. But that will come. Now for your problem, Mr. Talon."

"Yes. Mine. I told you the beginning. Now I'll tell you the end. Then I'll go back to the middle. On Sunday night, just about forty-eight hours ago, someone, several someones, killed my friend Carlee Desha and nearly killed me." For another hour, Talon explained. The old man did not seem nearly so interested in the story as he had been in surfing. He closed his eyes, nodded his head from time to time, and occasionally reached for the wineglass to take a sip. Talon spilled his classified-secret guts. The less interested he thought Ehrenzweig was, the more he struggled for facts. Finally, he had exhausted his intellect and his memory.

"We are lucky it is Tuesday night," the old man said.

"Huh?"

"Not 'huh?'—'why?'"

"Why?"

"Because Rod's is closed on Monday. Your timing was excellent, and I was hungry for the lobster. Shall we leave?"

"Yes." Talon felt drained and dejected. He paid the enormous freight and left a tip. They got back in the car, and the old man started to drive. Nothing was said until they arrived back at the train station. Then Ehrenzweig spoke.

"This is all very important, and I am not sure why."

Brilliant. Talon could feel the adrenaline flowing. "Yes."

"Let me tell you an amusing tale, Mr. Talon. I heard it as a story from the chief computer programmer for the N.R.O. It was not told to me on a confidential basis. I am sure that the national security interest in hushing it up was never mentioned."

The old man then told Talon of a mountain-climbing feat that made Hillary and Tenzing's conquest of Everest seem child's play. A climber, some years before, had successfully scaled a solid, sheer, eighty-foot face, using a construction-industry bolt-driver. He had suspended himself from fishing-line leader attached to the revolutionary pitons. Most probably, he had done it unassisted. There had been only three unfortunate aspects of his accomplishment. The human spider had killed himself through miscalculation on the way down. He had killed a guard intentionally. And the mountain was not a mountain at all, but the blank back wall of the secret N.R.O. computer building in Washington.

"Who was he?"

"Unknown. Untraceable. He was the perfect man who never was."

"What was he doing in there?"

"That was never discovered. He had his tools and so forth, a bit of the guard's blood splattered on him, and no more. It is merely a shot in the darkness, but perhaps you have provided a possible answer."

"Holy shit!"

"Please."

"Yes, sir."

"Another observation."

"Yes?"

"They were lying in wait for you."

"Yes."

"How did they know where you were?"

"I have no idea."

"Perhaps there are not too many ways back to the city?"

"No, but how would they know I was out on the Island?"

"Perhaps it was the traffic ticket."

"Oh."

"About your girlfriend, Miss Desha."

"Yes?"

"Did you carefully inspect her body?"

"No. She looked all broken up. She wasn't moving. Nothing. Absolutely nothing I could do for her."

135

"It seems rather strange that the police did not discover her body along with the other two. There was nothing in the paper. Just a thought."

"That's it?"

"The oracle has oracled." The old man smiled.

"Can I call you?"

"Anytime. We have a bargain, do we not?"

"Yes. But what about Sanroc? How could all this happen? That constant storm signal on R201?"

"Oh, that. It is quite simple, you realize. All it would require is an absolutely aberration-free computer comparison. First, a storm image match-up in the computer. If the computer memory at the N.R.O. shows a storm, and that is the same image it receives, there could never be an aberration."

"No."

"Secondly, a set of fact standards in the N.R.O. computer's memory bank supporting the image received is necessary. Say, one-hundred-percent cloud cover and large rainfall. That, as you've told me, is already in the N.R.O. factual or statistical memory. Correct?"

"Yes. The climber?"

"Perhaps. Thirdly, there would be the override."

"Override?"

"Oh, yes. Say, a tiny receiver built into Sanroc's telemetry circuits. At the end of each nine-day cycle, when Sanroc is disgorging its observations, a ground station would beam up the telemetry information for your R201 area. Then Sanroc would repeat it down to the receiver at the Goddard Space Flight Center in Maryland."

"So I'm going to have to go to Nepal to prove anything."

"Well, that would be one way. But completely unnecessary."

"I don't understand."

"The electrical override mechanism is in Sanroc. If you are

not a madman. But the transmitter would be somewhere here. In America. It is placed where it can beam up the information at precisely the time Sanroc is reporting back to the earth station. It's here, you see, near Goddard. Probably to the west, since Sanroc flies from west to east. It would have to be there in order to broadcast the false telemetry. That is, if you are correct and there is in fact something going on."

"Here."

"Yes. But only if you're right."

"Am I?"

"Perhaps. I think so."

"But to get the override into Sanroc and to at least set up the transmitter would take some kind of spy system here."

"Or perhaps a fail-safe device for the government, placed there to cover up things no one is to know. And being used or misused for that purpose. But, yes, some sophisticated system of people."

"In the government."

"Possibly. Hughes Aircraft built the Sanroc. Hughes does a lot of work for a lot of people."

"Thank you. *Auf Wiedersehen*," Talon said. It came out pretty good.

"*Auf Wiedersehen*," the old man said.

Talon noticed his ears were still ringing as he sat, alone and cold. He had to wait two hours for a train back to New York. He figured his brains were a little scrambled. Carlee. Alive? It seemed impossible. But where was her body? If he found the connections to his puzzle, maybe he'd find that out, too. That was the only way. Before they found him.

His seaman disguise was improving. He was starting to smell stale. He caught his train and slept to the end of the line.

37

Blue checked through Talon's Manhattan phone book with care, after a few drinks at his hotel. Several of the circled, checked or underlined numbers he was able to dismiss out of hand: sporting-goods, hardware and department stores, delicatessens, a motorcycle dealer, and some restaurants. Another was Talon's garage. Blue was left with some bars, which were appealing, and last, some names with first initials. Probably girls who wanted to avoid the inevitable obscenities a first-name listing would have produced. And the Hilton Hotel. At the Hilton, he could ogle the hookers, get some lubrication for his throat, check around and be only a few blocks from his own hotel.

He walked to the Hilton, asked the room clerk whether Talon had checked in, then retired to the bar for a lot of drinks over the next several hours.

It was kismet. If Talon had not done a double take and then waffled, Blue never would have tumbled. Blue was half in the bag as he was walking out of the Hilton, and Talon was inconspicuous in the New York menagerie. But Talon looked, and Blue shook off his alcoholic fog enough to spot a real pink elephant.

Talon was ready to bolt. Blue said, "Don't."

Talon dropped his sea bag and set up for hand-to-hand combat. So did Blue.

No one paid any attention except a security guard. He was watching the tableau as a relief to the spike-heeled dusky

ladies who took up most of his time. He gave Talon a light
tap on the top of the head to calm him down. It was enough.
Talon fell like a straw man.

38

"Maybe we'd better get a doctor," said Gray.

"He doesn't look so good," Blue slurred his words. It was
only by the grace of special government passes that they had
been able to get Talon into the building at Federal Plaza. It
was four in the morning. Blue was still more than a little
drunk. But he was feeling very much on top of the situation.

"That was a hell of a lucky connection."

Up yours, Blue thought. "Process of elimination."

"You're wilting my collar."

"There's nothing much we can do now. He's still out,"
said Blue.

"I still think we ought to call a doctor. He's a civilian, and
we're operating in the country. It could get hairy if he goes
sideways," said Gray.

"Quasi-civilian. I don't want anyone touching him until
we can get clearance. I'll take responsibility." He puffed up a
bit.

"That's easy to say, but I'm here, too."

"Go sleep."

"It's playing with fire. If he kicks, and someone picks up
on it, we could be in the soup. The whole Company."

"I said get out. I'll take the rap."

"He may die. He looks like he's in shock. He's got chills."

Gray eyed the form lying on the scanning table in Talon's old carrel. "Get him a blanket. There should be one in the ladies' lounge."

"All right."

"And put it in writing."

"What?"

"That you have made an independent decision to withhold medical attention from a seriously injured man, pending a decision from Langley."

Blue turned purple, but wrote up a note in longhand and signed it. Gray took the note, read it, and left.

Talon had heard the last bits of the conversation as the vultures hovered. The bureaucratic bastards are going to kill me, he thought. He wanted to ask them to get him a glass of water so he could pop a Darvon. He heard the southerner acknowledge receipt of the ass-protection note, and the door close as he left. There sure was no love lost between those two.

Blue eyed the huddled figure of Talon. He sniffed the stuffy air of the carrel. Without the air conditioner going, Talon came through ripe. Blue got up and went next door to wait for nine o'clock and orders.

Talon waited for a period he judged to be between half an hour and forever. He really needed the blanket, he thought. These snakes were perfectly willing to operate within the United States, screw over a citizen, and maybe let him die. They maybe wanted to kill him. But one thing he was sure of. They didn't sound as if they knew what was happening with Sanroc.

The flight reflex was pounding in his brain. The spirit willed, but the body was not responding. Where was the blanket?

Finally he managed to get his muscles moving. He pushed himself up. He assumed a sitting position on the scan table.

140

"Dangling" they'd called it at a hospital where he'd been with mono.

He'd laughed then. He dangled now. His contacts were clouded, gritty and dry. Opening his eyes was not going to be pleasant. He did, and it wasn't. He was waiting for the guy with the slurry-drunk voice to come with his blanket. Wrap it around me, he thought. I'll suck my thumb and lie down and rub the corner on my ear.

Blue had considered going in search of a blanket. Then he'd decided the freak could freeze for all he cared. And he didn't like Talon's smell, either. Blue went to the carrel he and Gray were working in. He pulled out a chair and wedged up the door to Talon's room. Then he went back to set up the polygraph they would use on Talon when he came around. Blue sat down. Ten seconds later he passed out like a guppy out of water, mouth open and gulping air.

Talon dangled some more, then got up. Shaky. He tried the door. Andy Alky had blocked it outside. It hardly moved. Talon put a weak shoulder to it. Nothing.

He looked over the carrel. There was a big pile of C.P.R.s on a hand cart. He took a quick peek. They were his. He leafed through them and found R201. The square storm was still there. He looked at Andy Alky's notes. Not a thing about the storm. And nothing much else about the most beautiful surfing spots in the world.

He pulled R201 out of the pile and put a big red X on it with a felt pen. He wrote a red "DUMBSHIT" on the notes and circled the analysis of R201. He tried to figure out why these guys were going through the C.P.R.s, when they should have at least some idea about what was happening. If they didn't, who would? He was too hurt and tired to give it much thought.

Talon reached into his pocket, took out a Darvon, and gagged it down dry. He was trapped. He sat down in front of the teletype and fired it up. He punched into Octopus, then routed through to the N.R.O. He hit the coordinates for R201 and addressed the computer, giving his code number. It didn't shut down.

He was still cleared for access. He sat and thought. And thought some more. He queried some more, asking little questions, searching for what he didn't know.

39

Down at Langley, a skeleton night crew tended the great data banks of Octopus. On a feedback line from the N.R.O., a signal was generated. It was on a newly programmed monitor circuit. A console flashed up a red light, and a high-speed printer started spitting out information:

```
R201 ADDRESSED, TALON CODE ACCESS.
ORIGINATION: GAMMA. LOCATION: GAMMA
OFFICE, FEDERAL PLAZA, NEW YORK CITY,
NEW YORK, USA. TIME: EST 4:53 . . .
```

It continued printing the questions Talon was asking. In a separate column it printed an analysis of the questions and the word patterns, all to confirm a connection with Talon. By the time the fifth line was printed, one member of the Octopus crew, puffy-faced and sallow from working her fifth continuous shift, was on the phone.

"Charley?"

"Yes."

"Miss Dawson here."

"Go ahead, Peg."

"It looks like he may be calling in from his section."

"In New York?"

"That's what I said."

"How the hell could he get in there?"

"All I'm giving you is what's come up here. Based on what we've got from Octopus, it's a good bet it's him."

"Before we move, I want more. I'm not going to call Mr. Bowles or take a chance on going in there without some kind of real confirmation. Then we can get an insider there right away."

"Sure thing. Can I go home now? I'm about to drop."

"No. Stay until we've got a positive I.D."

Just then he got all the confirmation he needed.

Talon had just punched in a question:

```
Q. GANJA PRODUCTION AREA R201, NEPAL.
GO.
    A. UNAUTHORIZED ACCESS. BYE.
```

The computer immediately shut down Talon's connection.

A buzzer sounded at Octopus. Miss Dawson shut it off, removed the last of the print-out, and got back to the phone.

"Hello?" she said.

"Yes. I'm still here. What happened?"

"He hit a key word: ganja. It's him. He's got it." She sounded very nervous. Self-preservation is a powerful motivator. At fifty-seven, her good days were long past, and she knew it. Tax-free money is fine, but in jail it's little comfort. She wondered whom she could talk to and tried to think of the word for what she needed. Immunity. She had missed the other side of the conversation while she thought of it. "What?"

"Hey, what's going on with you?"

"I'm scared."

"Oh." A warning bell no one else could hear went off in Charley's mind. "Let me go through it again. Erase the input, can the time-base-recorder tape, and sever the pickup program from the N.R.O. Shred the print-out and go home."

"Okay."

"Got it now?"

"Yes."

"Don't worry; it will all be fine. We'll get him."

She shuddered. Whom could she go see? "Okay."

40

Talon looked at his print-out. Ganja. The key. He knew it from the street. When it comes from Thailand, it's Thai-stick or Elephant. In other forms, from other places, it's called Colombian, kif, hemp, Kona gold, marijuana. How good it is depends on where it's from. Sunlight, soil conditions and rainfall are critical. Worldwide, there's nothing better than Nepalese ganja. So good it's a one-hit stone. Psychedelic and hallucinogenic, satisfying and anesthetizing.

Valuable. Elephant, tied on bamboo slivers, one hundred sticks to the pound, sells cheap at two thousand dollars a pound wholesale. Each of the sticks sells on the street for fifty dollars, easy. Five thousand dollars a pound retail. A bigger market than sliced bread. And ganja is better than Elephant.

People get killed in the import trade, lots of them. The money makes knives and guns seem reasonable. The dealers who have dealt retire to Mill Valley, Newport, or Laguna, in the Golden State, bury their tax-free money in hundred-dollar bills, and do a lot of dope and screwing. The good life.

Talon wished he had some smoke. The Darvon was working, but not so well. It was knocking him out a little. Ganja and the Company. He had to put that in the back of his mind somewhere. Soon he'd think about it. Right now, he wanted to pass out. But he had to move. Stay alive. Even if Andy Alky and the chickenshit from Mobile didn't know what the beef was, they were going to get him killed.

He pulled the sheet from the teletype and put it on top of the C.P.R.s. He circled it in red. He shouldered the door again. It didn't budge. He pulled one of the stiff C.P.R.s from the pile, slid it under the door, and tried to push away the chair in the hall. It didn't move. He looked around the office for a tool, a magic wand to take him to freedom. Nothing.

It was now five-fifteen. He was dying on his feet. If he didn't move, someone was going to do him in. And he didn't want to get done in.

He looked up at the ceiling. The air-conditioning duct, unlike those on the tube through which so many missions had been made possible, measured about six by ten inches. Nothing.

Five-twenty. He thought about starting a fire. Alarms go off. The New York Fire Department arrives and rescues. But by the time they arrived, he'd be a smoked salmon. Five twenty-five. His mind reeled. The Darvon didn't help the intellectual processes.

The ceiling. Those two-by-three-foot asbestos slabs were just hung on steel frames. The duct work for the air-conditioning system was up there along with God knew what else.

He put the chair on the table and climbed up. He pushed on a ceiling tile and stuck his head through. Enough light shone up to reveal a two-foot space between the hanging ceiling and the concrete floor above. It looked like the inside of a space vehicle, with pipes, ducts, and wires everywhere. But there was room to move.

He climbed back down. He dialed 911 and told the communications officer at the emergency police number that he was working the early shift and had seen a policeman in uniform get off the elevator at his floor. A short time later, he went on, he had heard gunshots and screams. He gave his name and said he had an identification card. He requested that the name be broadcast to the arriving police so he could avoid being shot for doing his civic duty. He gave the address and floor number.

Talon hung up. Somewhere he'd read that the only way to get action out of the N.Y.P.D. was to appeal to the cops' well-developed sense of self-preservation. He pulled his toilet kit out of the duffel bag and climbed into the ceiling space. He crawled along the metal false-ceiling hangers. The light got very dim, very quickly; only a bit filtered up through joints in the ceiling material. When he could go no farther, he lifted up a section and looked down.

He was over another carrel. This one was empty. He dropped his toilet case, let himself down, and stepped onto a table. He picked up the toilet case and walked out the door. He tried to remember what day it was. Wednesday.

He had been waiting in the elevator lobby no more than three minutes when one of the doors opened and two mean-looking plainclothes cops with badges pinned to their plaid hunting jackets stepped out, followed by a building guard. They had guns out and leveled at him.

"Drop it!"

"It's just my Doppkit. I'm Joseph Talon. I called in."

"I.D.?"

"Sure." Talon had his wallet ready. The building guard nodded at it, and the two toughies seemed satisfied. Another elevator opened, and some blue uniforms came out, rough and ready.

"Where are they?"

Talon pointed vaguely in the direction of the Company unit's area. "Thataway. I think the guy he was after was drunk."

"C'mon." The cowboys rode in for the kill. Talon got in one of the elevators and headed for freedom.

On the ground floor there were more uniforms, and he could hear sirens coming. One of the cops was fiddling with a two-way communicator.

"They may need help up there. They sent me down. I'm Joseph Talon." He flashed his wallet. One of them looked and grunted that Talon was okay. They all got into the elevator and went up.

Talon headed for the street. He walked out into a gaggle of N.Y.P.D. cars flashing red lights. What a fraternity. He wished he had someone to call. To protect him. He thought about Carlee.

He saw a citizen coming toward him, way down the block. Talon's first impulse was to turn and run. Three things stopped him. First, a natural aversion to panicky paranoia; second, the guy was black. So far, no one in his odyssey had varied from lily-white. Third, as the guy passed under a street lamp, Talon thought he recognized him as one of the security janitors. Probably going to work.

The man stopped about fifty feet away and pointed at him. Talon stopped walking and started to turn. So instead of catching Talon in the sternum and permanently assuaging his physical ailments, the bullet whipped through the pea coat, snicked across his ribs, and disappeared into the night.

Talon dropped and rolled, and heard more shots ringing out. He went over the curb into the gutter and scuttled under a parked *Daily News* truck. He was shaking and he was done.

He heard someone running toward him, then away. Then more shots. He didn't know for sure that he'd been hit, but he felt something.

Feet went running by him. In his white-knuckled hand, he held his kit. His only piece of the old life. His only possession. He couldn't take it anymore. He waited for death. He cried. He was reduced to nothing. A puddle of protoplasm, boneless, with death to come.

The executioner was, by then, lying flat on the sidewalk, his gun pointed at Talon's hiding place. It lay two feet away from the black hand which had held it. The man was dead, full of bullets. He was surrounded by blue uniforms.

"What the fuck was this scumbag doin'? We got half the cops in lower Manhattan here, for Chris'sakes," one cop said.

"Maybe it was one o' those ambushes. Remember those two cops in the Bronx a coupla' years back? Phone in a officer-in-trouble, then off a pig. The B.C.A.," said another.

"B.L.A. An' it don' look like dose muh'fuckers. Dis nigga's all 'lone." The only soul brother in the group took on an expert role.

"Well, call the meat wagon and the shooting squad. Who got 'im?" said a gold badge.

"Me."

"Me, too."

"I think I got a piece o' him."

"Okay. Check your weapons. Anyone with an empty casing, gimme the name and badge number." The gold badge walked away.

41

Talon heard some of the cop talk after his sobbing and shaking slacked off. Then he knew he wasn't going to die right there. Not right then. He put the collar of the pea coat in his mouth and bit down on it. And then he started crying again.

Soon there were more sirens, more flashing lights, more milling feet.

Talon tried to regain the urge to live. He just shook. He felt feverish. He was frightened, so frightened that he barely heard the noise or felt the cold of the pavement or smelled the New York smell in his nose, held fast to the street.

He was depressed, caring little for his physical integrity, no longer fearing death. Maybe desiring it. This wasn't the way it happened. Never. Nothing had ever prepared him for this. Deprivation and complete solitude were not in the American life-style. Robert Service had written of hunger that's not of the belly kind. Talon's hunger for physical comfort and an anchor point for his life reduced him to caring nothing about anything.

He had no friend. Nowhere to go. He was hurt. Head. Body. He gave up the remnants of his dinner with Ehrenzweig as quietly as possible. He became aware of a burning sensation across his left side, up high. His gut was empty. He felt the cold. The tears ran on the pavement. Nowhere to go. No one to go to.

42

Light mixed with the dark. Traffic moved outside the refuge he'd found. The truck started and moved away, rear differential grazing his shoulder, leaving grease and dirt and muck across the already soiled coat.

Talon lay there. Paralyzed, fetal. A car pulled up and honked at him, threatening his space, his time, his solitude in the Land of Nod. He'd seen the snake-haired Medusa and been turned to stone. Nothing would move him.

"Are you all right?"

Nothing.

"Please, are you all right?"

"Go away. I'm dead. Inside, outside," Talon said.

"I thought you were."

"Get away. Don't talk to strangers. New York." He kept his eyes shut.

"They'll arrest you or a car'll run you over."

"Right." He opened his eyes. Still the haze. There was a reasonably young, unreasonably ugly girl, with glasses all over her face. Her nose was about three inches away from his face.

"Come on." She tugged at his coat. "You're bleeding. Your jacket's soaked."

"Good Samaritans get screwed."

"I wish." She tugged him up onto the curb, then to his feet. He shuffled into gear. "Goodbye," she said.

"Right." Someone caring helped tip the scale back a bit away from death by resignation. He walked away in a fair approximation of a Bowery muscatel ramble. And the Bowery was where he ended up. Not so different from any of the regulars.

He found an empty alley, and he stuffed his wallet and all his money, except for twelve dollars, into his right sock. He took off the pea coat and draped it over his left shoulder, covering the wet spot. He held it close to his body with his left arm.

He walked the Bowery. He finally stopped under a white six-by-six-foot sign proclaiming the Quincy Hotel, a Lyons House. It was one fleabag in the chain of fleabags which dotted the skid row of all skid rows.

He stepped in and paid three dollars and eighteen cents for a single room. The counter man never looked at him, and would have seen only the familiar stubble, dirt, gaunt features, and emmet stare if he had.

"Soap?"

"Right."

"Big?"

"Right."

The other man waited.

Talon's mind raced. What was going on? Finally, lazily, he reached in his pocket, pulled out a dollar and handed it over. Then he waited.

Finally, Talon got a hotel-size bar of no-name soap and sixty cents change.

He opened the door to his room, walked in, and propped a chair against the knob. He vaguely realized the healthy nature of the return of his interest in self-preservation.

The next thing he did was to lie down on the bed. He reached into his pocket with his grimy right hand and found a Darvon. He managed to swallow it. Then he closed his eyes and started his mantra. He pumped all the ki he could into that certain central point in his belly. Half an hour later, he did not want to open his swollen eyes. But he did.

He took the ragged towel hanging on the back of the door and pressed it against his side. He took the room key, his toilet kit, and the bar of soap. He stepped into the hall and hunted up the washroom. It looked like a sewer line had backed up. The door had no lock, so he went back to his room and got the chair.

Securing the bathroom door with the chair seemed to work. He stripped off his clothes and looked at himself in a broken, partially silvered mirror. His hands and face were so filthy that he looked like Jolson in blackface. He decided not to clean up his face. He'd survive. The hands he had to get scrubbed.

The bullet had stripped out a furrow of skin, fat, and flesh about two inches long. The tape with which he'd bound up the original rib damage was frayed around the wound. It was soaked with new blood, caked with old.

He tore the tape away from the wound. That started some fresh bleeding. Then he cleaned it with the soap and lots of water. It hurt, but it was positive.

Someone started pushing, then banging on the door. After a while the noise stopped.

Talon finished washing. He dried off the wound and the surrounding tape. He dabbed at the new blood with paper towels. He washed out his sweater in the sink, and watched the stains from his blood mix with the murky tap water. He washed under his arms. He wrapped the towel around his chest, put his gear in the kit, and flushed the bloody stuff. He pulled the chair away from the door.

Whoever had been knocking had left what he was knocking about in the hall.

Talon walked back to his room, dragging the chair and being careful not to move too much. He jammed the door shut with the chair and tried to relax. He waited until the blood stopped welling up from his side; then he stripped off some of the tape from lower down. He used it to pull the edges of the wound together. Then he slowly stretched out on the bed and fell asleep.

43

"Twelve hours in the goddamn tank! Why the fuck couldn't you get me out?" Blue was green around the gills. He had a mouse under his left eye, and the left side of his face was swollen. His head felt bad from the enthusiasm of the cops who had found him wandering in the federal office complex, gun in hand.

"You're lucky they didn't pop you for good," Gray drawled. "Talon really got you with your pants down."

"If you hadn't said to get the goddamn blanket, I never would have left him."

"Sure. He must have been quick as a cat."

The sarcasm was lost on Blue, who was nursing his wounds and feeling terrible. "The bastard is brilliant. Those cops really worked me over."

The cab they were riding in stopped at the Federal Plaza. Gray paid. The cab driver sniffed at the quarter tip for the three-dollar ride. He took a look at the passengers and decided to keep it to himself.

"How the hell could he get away? There must have been a thousand cops there," Blue said.

"He created a lot of confusion. The only thing missing was air support. Anyway, we identified the inside man here."

"How's that?" Blue stopped at the elevator bank and talked in a low voice.

"A janitor, security-cleared by us, who worked the Company sector up there, got shot. He was down in the street shooting at the cops."

"Part of the diversion?"

"Seems that way. Talon could have called him for cover. Anyway, they made him into Swiss steak. We're doing a check on him now. But right away, I can tell you something's funny. I visited his apartment in Greenwich Village this morning, and besides supporting a white boyfriend, he had a little Taj Mahal going."

"Banks?"

"We're checking now. I've got someone standing by to go along. He had a safe-deposit key, and the police are getting court orders. Anyway, I think your workout with them wouldn't have been so bad if all the shooting down in the street hadn't started."

Blue couldn't figure out how the guy looked so fresh all the time. Blah, blah, blah, that halfassed southern drawl popped out facts and conclusions. It was annoying as hell. He wanted to strangle Gray and that bastard Talon. "Well, let's go up."

"One more thing. No one at Langley was very happy with the escape. You might try to find him again. It doesn't look good. Plus, the cops are asking a whole lot of questions."

Here, I capture Talon through good work and get no credit, Blue thought. This southern creep takes off, and who gets jailed, beat up and called down? "Sure. What about the capture?"

"They figure pure luck. After all, you'd been in that bar at the Hilton four hours straight."

Blue's gut was turning over. "I'd better check out that carrel where we left him."

"I doubt we'll find anything. But let's look."

They got on the elevator.

Miss D'Arcy was waiting for them just outside Talon's carrel. "You guys are like a herd of elephants. This whole place was crawling with cops. And that poor Mr. Daniels who got shot. What's going on here?"

She turned to Blue. "Your eye looks like the inside of a clamshell. Poor boy. Who hit you?"

"Everyone." Boy. She couldn't be over thirty-five, and he was pushing fifty.

"Sure. How did he get out?" she asked.

I wish I'd never found him in the first place, Blue thought. "I don't know. When I checked the carrel, the chair was still outside the door, like I left it. I looked in, and he was gone. Then the plainclothes cops were there. I thought they were confederates."

"Through the ceiling," Gray said. "He went up through one of those asbestos tiles and came down in another carrel. Then he met the cops, showed them his I.D. and left, presumably to meet the nigga'."

"Daniels?" asked Miss D'Arcy.

"Guess so," said Gray.

"Looks like," said Blue.

"What would our janitor have to do with Talon?" asked Miss D'Arcy.

Blue found himself wanting to look at Gray for the go-ahead to relate the theoretical connection between Talon and someone on the inside. Blue hated Gray even more because the woman noticed. "The eyes and the bug," he said.

"I know about the bug," she said, "but what about the eyes?"

"Someone wants Talon—besides us. Someone pimped the major newspapers to print a story. . . ."

"Not the police?" she asked.

"We thought so originally, but—" He looked reflexively at

Gray. Shit. "But we spotted the fact that they had the wrong eye color in the description. Talon wears brown contacts over blue eyes. It's on his driver's license."

"Oh," she said.

"It adds up to an insider. Wrong eye color by someone who'd seen him."

"Oh," she said. "Mr. Daniels."

"We think."

"What else is going on?" she asked, getting into the spirit of things.

"The . . ."

"Later," said Gray, taking over with a word. He said it with a drawl.

Blue deflated. But he extricated himself gracefully. "We're still checking."

"I think we'd better look at his carrel, if you don't mind, ma'am," said Gray.

"Why, no. Go right in. I've just been waiting here for you."

"While we're doing that, I wonder if you'd call Langley to set up a stakeout team at the Hilton, ma'am? He was probably there for something, and I certainly want to cover all the bases."

Blue groaned inside.

Then they checked the carrel carefully. They didn't find a thing except Talon's battered bloodstained bag, full of battered clothes.

44

When Talon awoke, it was dark. He heard some traffic outside. He felt his ear. It had quit leaking. He checked his watch. It had stopped. He wound it and sat up on the saggy sprung bed and meditated. He concentrated on the area in the center of his forehead where his third eye was.

Half an hour later he stood up, turned on the bare overhead bulb and felt for a mooring for his mind. His body aches were there still. But they had become a part of him, a point of reference for whatever life he still had. His chest felt somewhat better. But the perpetual headache was pounding. Even more when he strained at anything.

He managed to get down the last Darvon. Then he pulled the chair from the doorknob, sat on it, and started to think.

There were two areas of concern that he was able to identify. He felt that if he could settle on an approach to these, his discomfort might abate. There was an overall depression to his mood, less perhaps than the shell-shocked waves of nausea and hysteria that had gripped him when he was under the truck, but still enough.

So he attacked the present. Giving perspective to the areas of concern was the way to some semblance of sanity. He struggled with it.

First, his body. Second, the reason they were trying to kill him.

He found that his cynically good-natured approach to life had gone south while he was cheek down, hugging the ground. The combination of losing ingredients called despair, depression, and hopelessness had replaced his life spirit. His mind didn't feel sharp or creative. Part of this he could attribute to exhaustion and the physical abuse he'd suffered, part to the terrors and losses he'd faced. The latter would require a long-term program of mental rejuvenation. So he narrowed the field to the present considerations for the preservation of his mortal body.

He had been through serious shock, and survived. He had sustained a brain concussion, a possible fractured skull, broken ribs, and a gunshot wound. He had survived. But the effects had been devastating. He was very weak, his coordination was terrible, and he needed healing.

He needed to have this hellish excursion done. Finished. He had all the information he was going to get. But he was not physically able to take the giant step of putting it together to get the answers. Later. Maybe it would be solved by then. Whatever had happened was and always had been out of his control. Elephants can have fleas, he thought, but fleas can't have elephants. He was a flea, and they—whoever "they" were—they were elephants.

His mind came back to reality. He shifted himself back to the bed, after replacing the chair under the doorknob. Fleas and elephants. Later.

He recalled the book he'd gotten when he'd been living on his boat in Santa Cruz. Was that him? He thought of the hammock he'd strung between the mainmast and the mizzen shrouds. Warm evenings he'd swing on it, easy in the light harbor swell, with a glass full of ice cubes and white California grape. Soon some chick would wander by and . . . Carlee . . .

He switched back to where he was. He knew his mind had gone wandering again. What was it? Right, the book. *Ship's Medicine Chest*. He'd fantasized sailing to Tahiti. He had read books on navigation, cruising, and first aid. Ah, Talon, he thought, the dreams. Wherever did they go? *Tempus fugit,* all right.

Back to the book. Ribs, fractured? Sharp pains may be relieved with sufficient pressure. Bind with adhesive tape. Done. Rest.

He figured he'd slept perhaps twelve or fourteen hours. But he didn't feel rested. The effects of his feeling of depression and the pain of his body had combined to rob him of real rest. He thought of his pre-sleep moments aboard his yawl *Truant.* Funny, her name had escaped him until just then. The tiny harbor waves slapping against her hull, little washing sounds in the dead-still nights.

The book. Skull, fractured? Brain, concussed? Watery, bloody discharge from ears; headaches; dizziness; faintness? Immediate hospitalization, x-rays. Rest.

He was working hard at keeping his attention on the physical problems. His mind continued to flit across a spectrum of thoughts. He decided that the images flashing by his brain in a kaleidoscopic array were too jumbled to allow him deep concentration. He needed that concentration to work on "them." But that would be later.

Rest. That was the answer. Neither the body nor the spirit was willing. Maybe next week, he'd go out into the world again. Rest now.

He got up, made sure the chair was wedged tightly against the doorknob, and turned out the light. He got back on the bed. He got into the most comfortable position he could figure out. He closed his eyes. Rest, he thought to himself. Rest. That'll do it. Then I can go and beard the lion in his den. After the den gets located.

He was almost asleep when he opened his eyes and his mind went into a panic. Wednesday gone. Tomorrow's Thursday—or is it? He wasn't sure of the days. He counted back. The nine-day Sanroc cycle would end on Friday, and all the information would be radioed back to the earth station in the late afternoon, as Sanroc flew by. The aberration processing by computer comparison would begin then.

After the completion of the present Sanroc cycle, they would be safe for another nine days to concentrate on one thing—hunting for him. Talon felt that his life expectancy was counted in minutes, not days. He had the whole Company, the New York police, and the others after him. "Them."

He had to move. He had the option to run for good. He considered it. He thought about his possessions at his apartment—his records, his surfboard. Not worth it. Running was better than dying. He thought about Carlee, and recanted. What the hell, he thought, life ain't all that much.

He called to his subconscious mind for a two-hour nap. He needed rest; he needed life; but, far more, he needed a resolution.

Then he slept.

45

"Talon has disappeared, and Peg Dawson is in a complete panic, Mr. Bowles."

"Let's not get in a snit, Charles. You know how women are. She's probably in premenstrual turmoil. Anyway, we have a man watching her. Have another drink, and for God's sake keep your own head on your shoulders." He signaled to a waiter and settled back comfortably in his seat. His Silver

Springs, Maryland, club was posh enough to provide chairs that made a slouch worthwhile. "We will nail Talon and allay Miss Dawson's fears with a handsome payment, and our proprietaries will continue to exist quite nicely. The kitchen may be hot, but, after all, isn't that what it's all about?"

"This one guy who picked Talon up . . ."

"The drinker?"

"Yes. He and the other one are putting things together. They may come up with something." He shifted nervously, pulling his pants up again at the knees and leaving too much material rucked up around the thighs. His underarms were dripping, and he had trouble connecting the rim of his glass with his mouth.

"The drinker I've known for years, Charles. He is a toady, slow and unsure. The pickup, I am certain, was the result of luck and superstition rather than skill and dexterity. However, I feel that he is the more dangerous of the two. He is a plodder. And he does have experience. I had hoped that the match-up between him and the young southern go-getter would provide sufficient infighting to eliminate effective intellectualization. I still feel it will."

"Yes," said Charley. Every time someone said the word "toady," he felt uncomfortable. He started to think about early retirement and mentally added up his chips.

"Really, Charles, you must listen. You are in a trance."

"Yes, Mr. Bowles." Charley regained the present with an effort.

"Our search for Talon will be successful. It was a stroke of genius that the remainder of our team in New York picked up the girl's body. If there was any depth in that relationship, there's a good chance Talon will surface to look for her. Regardless, he must make his debut at some point. And naturally we will be there. Of course, if that pickaninny hadn't bungled the job, we'd be better off." He sighed and looked perfectly bored with the whole thing.

The boredom had no calming effect on Charley. For thirty-two years in the Company, he had seen Ivy League yawns decide the fate of people and nations. Humility and fear were depressing little peccadillos to those types. And they still made lots of mistakes. "We'll do better next go-round, Mr. Bowles," he said.

"Let's hope for that."

The audience was over. Charley gulped the rest of his drink and left. Bowles stepped into the card room for his afternoon bridge game. He played chess the rest of the time. With live pawns.

46

It was dark when Talon woke up. He was fairly sure he had not slept around the clock to Thursday night, but not certain. He felt a momentary panic. He got control over himself and sat up. He was very stiff, and the pain messages from his body to his brain were loud and clear.

He forced himself to meditate. He knew intellectually that he could say the mantra or "Coca-Cola" to himself and the same result would be obtained. He would sink into his subconscious mind and achieve a deep state of rest. But the hundred and twenty-five smackers he'd shelled out to the Maharishi persuaded him to go along with the more mystical aspects of a very simple psychophysiological process.

He finished the meditation. He felt ready to cope with the

immediate problems. He turned on the light, gathered his possessions, and went to the washroom. He took care of his needs, washed his face, and put in his contacts. He went downstairs. A different front-desk man was on duty in the cage. He was doing a tongue-hanging doze.

"Hey," Talon said.

"Wha . . ." The bowery type opened a pair of eyes. One was opaque, the other fishy and bloodshot.

Great morning face, thought Talon. "What time is it?"

"Look at the clock." He pointed up. "Ya blind?"

"Sorry. What day?"

"Day?"

"Thursday? Friday?"

"What do I look like, the Answer Man? How the fuck should I know what day? I work nights." He started to close his eyes again.

"I have to pay for another night. Get my card."

"Name?"

"How should I know? Second floor, Room G." Talon showed him the key.

The man pulled Talon's registration card. "Well, what day did ya come in?"

"Wednesday morning."

"Ya pay for more 'n one day?"

"Nope."

"Well, ya dummy, ya think this is a charity? If ya paid for the room, it's yours. If ya didn't pay, ya go out on ya ass."

"So it's Thursday."

The clerk's eyes turned at Marty Feldman angles. Exasperation turned to malice. "Sure, ya fuck. It's four-thirty in the A.M., Thursday. Ya gonna pay for another day or are ya just gonna stay here and ask me questions?"

"Pay." Talon handed over four dollars and scooped up his change.

The clerk immediately went to sleep. Talon walked outside and found a White Tower. He choked down a lot of grease and onions inside a couple of buns, had two cups of coffee and fifteen minutes of deep-fat-fryer air. He had planning to do and less than thirty-six hours to see it reach fruition.

47

Talon sat on the chair in his room and thought. There was no more time for his body. If he failed, he was sure he would find plenty of rest during the nine days following Friday. Like forever. The pieces—where were they all?

He wanted to know whether his scrawl on Blue's notes and the print-out and his red X on R201 had meant anything to them. But he couldn't call. He had no one to trust. The only time he'd know for certain would be if the Sanroc override were shut down. Then everyone would know.

It had to be an illicit operation. No question. The key word "ganja" had told him that. It had to be big-time, and it had to have plenty of money and people involved. And it was happening under the cover of an intelligence operation. Maybe the Company. Probably the Company.

He couldn't come out. Everyone was after his tail. The good guys thought he'd turned, and the bad guys had his number. They all wanted him gone.

He thought about barricading himself somewhere and spilling his guts to Flynn. But Flynn might be in on it. More likely they'd spill his guts for him. Talon looked at his watch. Six-twenty A.M. Time was flying by.

Maybe write a letter. To whom? No one was going to believe him. If anyone did, that person was dead, too. What value life, Talon? If he came out, he was probably dead. Same if he didn't. But he wanted life, wanted that last chance to find the wave of his dream.

Okay, so he had to come out. Where? And how could he find the linchpin for this mess? Pull it and he could set "their" intricate machinery to work grinding itself to bits. But coming out into the world against the type of army they could field was suicide.

Think, Talon. Six forty-five.

A stalking-horse. A cover, a mask. He tried to put one together in his mind.

48

He went downstairs later, got some grudging change from the cockeyed clerk, and found a pay phone in working order a few steps from the flophouse.

"Hello," a reasonably wide-awake man's voice on the other end answered.

At least he hadn't disturbed the whole house. "Hello, is Dr. Ehrenzweig, Senior, there?"

"And who is calling?" The voice sounded amiable enough, with perhaps a trace of Wagner in it.

"Tell him it's the gentleman from the *Daily News,* please. He will know."

"Just a moment, please."

Enough time went by for the operator to demand an additional deposit. Talon requested a charge reversal. When

Dr. Ehrenzweig answered, he seemed annoyed by the operator's request for confirmation. Finally he agreed to accept the balance of the phone charges.

"Mr. Talon?"

"Right, er, yes."

"Our understanding did not, I think, include the acceptance of long-distance charges, Mr. Talon."

"Trust me."

"Shall I?"

"Yes."

"Well, proceed."

Talon thought that Ehrenzweig sounded gruffer than he really was. "They almost killed me again. I have decided to give myself up and hope I can save my skin."

"I don't believe you."

"About the killing?"

"The giving up."

"You know me. You also know what I'm up against. I must get this message across to you exactly right. They may put you on a polygraph. You must remember *everything* about this call."

"I'm starting to see. . . ."

"Please don't. Don't think about it. This may put you in great danger."

"I think not. Regardless, there is the surfing. Our bargain for the lessons holds?"

"Yes, Doctor."

"Continue."

"Nothing of our prior conversation must be mentioned, or our meeting. It would put you in great danger."

"Yes."

"Here it is. Contact someone in Security in the missile program. The Company will be swarming all over you in short order. Say that I will give myself up tomorrow morning. I will not tell you where I am. Give them all the details of the call . . ."

"Except the caveat with respect to our prior meeting."

"Yes. Say I picked you out of a book at the New York Public Library. Main branch."

"You did, so that is true."

"Yes, I did. I will give myself up to you tomorrow morning at the Grand Central Station information counter."

"I have that exactly."

"Off the record again. If the override exists, you said the ground station would be close to the actual receiver at Goddard?"

"I said so."

"Thank you, my friend. *Auf Wiedersehen.*"

"*Auf Wiederhören.* Talon?"

"Yes?"

"Take care. I pray that you will be alive tomorrow."

Talon hung up. He bought a *New York Times* and a pack of Kools. He went back up to his room and thought out the rest of his plan. It was seven-thirty. He had a very few hours to get the first phase on track. He lit up and scanned the ads in the classified section under "Motorcycles."

49

"Mr. Bowles!" An excited voice pierced Bowles's sleep-in morning.

"Yes, Charles. I'm *hors de combat* with a touch of the flu." He sounded very bored, even as he sniffed the air in his Georgetown home for smells of breakfast cooking. He had meant to get up at ten-thirty anyway, and it was just a few minutes before.

"Talon has made contact. With Dr. Ehrenzweig of NASA."

"Who?"

"One of the kraut retreads who slid in with Von Braun. Some kind of satellite expert."

Bowles became more interested. "What did he say?"

"Talon or Ehrenzweig?"

"Charles, after all, you didn't talk to Talon, did you? Obviously, I want to know what Ehrenzweig reported of his conversation with Talon." His exasperation came through loud and clear.

"Oh. Well, he said that Talon was going to give himself up to him, Ehrenzweig, tomorrow morning at Grand Central Station."

"Where is Talon?"

"He didn't say, but . . ."

"Ehrenzweig or . . ."

"Talon didn't say."

"Did he tell this Ehrenzweig anything else?"

"No, I don't think, but . . ."

"Don't think? Look, we have to move on this. Now. Get Talon and remove him from the scene before we get a public display. We must keep an eye on that inept alcoholic boob we have working up there in New York. Get one of our people in on this thing. Do you understand?"

"Yes, sir. But I was trying to say that they think they may have a line on how to get Talon."

"Oh, well. Good. Keep me advised. Goodbye." Bowles hung up the phone. He sniffed the air again and detected a hint of bacon. It made him feel much better.

50

The call about Ehrenzweig had come into the carrel at eight-twenty. Gray was seated, laboriously poring over a coincidence-point computer run of the Talon case. Blue was in a bit of a haze because of heavy libation and little sleep on Wednesday night. Gray took the call. Blue did not bother going for the phone anymore. His star was descending.

Gray put the phone down and gave the import of it to Blue in twenty-five words or less. He took off ten minutes later from the Wall Street heliport for Summit, New Jersey. Blue was left to hold the fort, which seemed rather more like a bag.

They had found nothing in Talon's carrel the day before, except for the old clothes in the canvas bag. Something was at the back of Blue's mind, niggling away. He tried to think about it, then went to the carrel to look. Nothing.

He had started to walk out when he remembered. The notes he'd taken on Talon's extra C.P.R. orders were gone. Shit. He'd have to redo them. Well, it was something to pass the time while Gray came home with the bacon.

The top C.P.R. was wrinkled up. Blue didn't remember doing that, so he scanned it carefully. Nothing he could detect. He checked the coordinates from a list he had, giving the location. Hermosa Beach. Tits and surf. Big deal.

The rest of the C.P.R.s went fast, simply because he'd already been through them once and found nothing. When he had finished the list, comments and locations, he discovered that one was missing. At nine thirty-five, just as he had pinpointed R201 as the one that had vanished, the phone rang. It was Gray.

"I'm with Ehrenzweig. I've got the whole story."

"Do we have Talon?" asked Blue.

"Well," Gray drawled, "I might just."

The bastard, Blue thought. I'm going to wring his neck. "What is it?"

"Check with the phone company. Talon called long-distance. Ehrenzweig's number is 201-935-6244."

Now I got him. "How the hell do you expect to get anything? The only record will be at Talon's end of the call. Probably a pay phone."

"Well . . . you're right, but . . ." Gray drew it out.

The fucker, he's got me. I'll kill him, Blue thought. "Yes?"

"Talon ran out of change. Ehrenzweig accepted charges on the balance of the call."

Blue wanted to bite the knuckle he had jammed between his teeth. A few seconds passed before he could speak. "I'm working on something here, too. One of Talon's C.P.R.s is missing."

"Can it, Yank. I got that ol' boy by his short hairs. I'll be coming right back. So follow up on that number, hea'?"

Blue hung up. He sat and burned. Then he called the telephone company.

Telephone toll records are one of the most valuable sources of intelligence. A computer will reveal who made a call, to whom, the date, time, charges and duration. It will even do complex phone-number comparisons to tie people together. The order Blue had was much simpler.

By ten forty-five, when Gray arrived back, the Company was already mobilizing its forces in the lower Manhattan area, with the nominal support of the F.B.I. for cover.

By eleven-ten, the whole entourage of lawmen was gathered in the general area of Talon's hostel, watching, making inquiries. At noon a final positive identification of

Talon was made. He was the man in Room G on the second floor of the Quincy Hotel. According to the clerk, Talon was still up there. Gray spoke with the room clerk personally. Blue stood around.

By a few minutes after twelve, the whole block was covered. Agents decked out in dirt and rags nearly outnumbered the flies. They settled down to wait.

Gray sent a man up to the room with an electric stethoscope. He reported back to Gray at a storefront operations center right across the street.

"He's in there," the agent said. "I heard him through the door. It sounds like he's asleep."

That was what Gray wanted to hear. He called down to Langley for further instructions.

Blue was really in the background now. He was just there for backup. He tried to interest Gray in the missing C.P.R. on a couple of occasions, and failed.

By that time another representative from Langley was on the scene. Situated in a room three buildings over and two floors up, he had a clear field of fire at the Quincy with a short-barreled Ruger .44-magnum rifle. The powder loads for the bullets had been reduced to lower the muzzle velocity below the speed of sound, which would make the silencer work just fine. The big piece of lead the Ruger threw would do a great job. He had powerful Smith & Wesson night-view binoculars, just in case. He was ready for Talon. He was Charley's man.

51

At ten-forty that Thursday morning, a messenger from Blue Streak Services walked into the New York Hilton and collected Talon's bags. The messengers in New York are either black or Puerto Rican, or old, white and retired. Mostly the last, like this one.

Talon watched the old man leave the Hilton, struggling with the two bags. He saw a driver help him load the bags into a cab. Talon was in another cab just across the street. He was scrunched down in the back, trying to be invisible. After ten minutes of watching, he asked the driver to take him to the Port Authority bus depot.

Talon got out of the cab and paid. He was wearing a terribly ripe, frayed black coat. It had cost him half a gallon of Thunderbird.

He waited through minutes he didn't have and couldn't afford. Eleven-thirty. He didn't see any Company types around. He took a deep breath, turned up his collar, and shuffled in.

The old errand boy was standing at the Greyhound ticket counter. He was looking around. Talon carefully observed the area. At least the north and south pro team wasn't there. Not so far as he could see, anyway. Talon made his way over to the messenger, pausing a few moments as a long line of little children marched along two by two, holding hands. Teachers were clucking. They were going on an outing. He wished that he were that young again, not hunted by the world and haunted by Carlee.

"I'm Mr. Cooper." Talon had a folded twenty in the hand

he held out, palm up. "You have the keys?"

"You?" said the messenger.

"Me."

"Sure."

The man took the twenty and handed over two locker keys with red plastic grips. He tried not to look at Talon.

Talon knew why. Three days of beard, the coat, the smell, and his toilet kit wrapped in a wrinkled brown paper bag, like a bottle of booze, didn't stimulate interest. He told the messenger to wait awhile before leaving.

Talon had about six hundred and seventy-five dollars left. And a little change. He sat on a bench and everyone moved away, looked away. He was shaking. He waited for "them." They didn't come.

He walked over to the lockers and found the one that matched the number on one of his keys. He opened it and took out the computer terminal.

He found the other locker and removed his suitcase. He took both it and the terminal to the men's room. He checked for feet and stepped into an empty stall, locking it behind him.

He had half-expected to find a neat little homing device secreted with his gear. None there. He took out the check protector and the encoder. He used the encoder to put the Company account number on the bottom of two Irving Trust checks and used the check protector to handsomely and officially print "six hundred and thirty-eight dollars" on one, "nine hundred and forty-four dollars" on the other. He signed and countersigned both checks in different hands and inks. They looked fine. He stepped out of the toilet and found an electrical outlet above the sinks. He plugged in the computer terminal and typed his name on the checks as payee. Local traffic didn't give him a glance. Thank God for New York. He went back into his stall.

Time was going by too fast. He checked his watch. He had to be at Seventieth Street and Broadway at one o'clock. His temples were pounding. An hour and ten minutes was all he had.

He took his toilet kit out of the paper bag. He closed up the suitcase, left it, and went to a sink. He washed his face and then shaved carefully, leaving the beginnings of his moustache intact. He looked better. He went back into the stall.

He opened his suitcase. He took out his Armalite rifle, a spare clip, his homemade silencer, and a box of .22 shells, and put them in the paper bag with his toilet kit. He closed the suitcase and picked it up, along with the computer terminal and paper bag. He left the tatty coat in the stall and walked out of the men's room.

He found an open locker. He put in his suitcase, dropped in a couple of quarters, and pocketed the key. He thought about pumping in another fifty cents to store the computer terminal. He decided to lay some largesse on one of the citizens of New York. He left it there in an open locker. He'd give it fifteen minutes.

He walked out with his paper bag, looking at his watch. He now had fifty minutes.

Talon hailed a cruising cab and told the driver to head uptown on Sixth Avenue. He checked behind him. Nothing. They proceeded uptown until he spotted a men's store. He paid off the driver and got out.

He bought a shearling-lined leather jacket, a white turtleneck sweater, a tee shirt and a pair of Britannia denim bells. He wore them out of the store and canned the parcel of his old clothes in an overflowing wastebasket at Sixth and Central Park South. He looked better and felt better with the new clothes on.

Four hundred and twenty-three dollars left. Twenty minutes left.

He got a cab and arrived at Seventieth and Broadway on time.

52

One of the hard cases from Langley came in to report to Gray at a little after noon. "The boys are getting nervous out there," he said.

"I just had the electronics guy put a spike mike into the adjacent room," Gray said. "Talon's still in there, sleeping."

"Shouldn't we go in?"

"Ten minutes. I'll wait here and observe."

"Okay," said the hard guy.

Bullshit, thought Blue. He was listening, while remaining on the periphery of the discussion. The damn politician is going to hang back in case there's a screw-up. If it goes right, he'll get the credit. He never misses a step.

"I wanted to wait to see if there were any conspirators we could snag, but we'll get that out of him anyway," Gray said to no one in particular.

Sure, thought Blue. Redneck was just wracking his pinhead to see whether there was any way he'd forgotten to protect his ass.

Precisely ten minutes later, the street was sealed off. The ragtag army of dirt-smudged Company aces moved in on the Quincy Hotel.

Blue wandered out onto the sidewalk to watch the action.

A few minutes later, two of the operatives appeared, supporting a filthy Thunderbird-reeking wino between them. The object of their quest was wearing Talon's pea coat. He was protesting loudly out of a toothless mouth.

Blue was about to yell at them when he heard some faint

175

thunking noises. He saw one of the Company men lurch backward as the wino dropped like an empty sack. Blue perked up.

Gray came out of the store like Jessie Owens, almost knocking Blue over. Blue didn't mind one bit.

Blue wandered over to the clot of men surrounding their wounded comrade and dead quarry. Some split off to try to locate the sniper. Others went back into the Quincy to break doors.

Just as Blue got there, Gray said, "Shit."

Blue agreed and walked away smiling.

53

"Nice bike," said Talon.

"Practically new," the nervous nineteen-year-old boy said.

They were standing on the sidewalk appraising a '73 B.S.A. It was stock, and the mileage was low. Images of Carlee and his own burning Beezer flashed through Talon's mind. "Run good?" he said.

"Like new. Better. The only thing I changed was the bars—I put on high-risers. More comfortable riding, huh?"

Talon checked the bike carefully. It looked good. "You want eleven-fifty?"

"Yes."

"Take ten-fifty?"

"No. It's worth twelve. It's cherry."

"I want to ride it. Check it out."

"Well, I don't know. I've only got one hat. I'd sort of want to go with you."

"Tough to get the feel unless I'm solo, eh? Now, here's what I'll do. I'll give you this check and a hundred to hold, and we'll haggle over the difference when I get back. If it's okay, we'll go cash the check."

He produced the rubber nine hundred and forty-four dollars.

"I don't know . . ."

"Do you have the ownership?" Talon tried to shift the burden of proof.

"Sure, right here."

Talon took the pink slip and made a big thing out of comparing the engine and frame numbers. "Looks okay."

"Sure it is. You got I.D.?"

Talon showed him his driver's license and Ag identification card.

"Looks okay," the kid said. "All right, try it." He reached out and retrieved the pink slip.

Talon pulled on the helmet. It was a little tight, but it would do. He got on the bike. He punched the carburetor juicers, flipped the key, and got ready to kick the crank and fire up.

"Hey! Wait!" The kid looked like he was going to back out. Seller's remorse. He was knocking on the top of the helmet.

Talon thought about a quick stiff-arm. But if the bike didn't catch right away, he could have problems. Especially with the paper bag between his legs. The kid had a couple of shock cords around the saddle, but Talon didn't want to look too permanent—yet.

"Yes?" Talon said amiably.

"The check . . ."

Shit, Talon thought. He's going sideways.

"You didn't endorse it."

"Right. A simple matter." Talon fumbled for a pen. He'd left his in the suitcase. Finally the kid produced one, and Talon laid the check on the tank and endorsed it. The kid looked concerned. "I didn't press hard," Talon said.

"Okay. Remember, I didn't promise anything under eleven-fifty."

"Right."

"Five minutes?" the kid said hopefully.

"Ten at the most."

Talon took off uptown. At Eighty-sixth he turned west, stopped the bike, and fastened the paper bag down behind him. Permanent.

The kid was still pacing around, holding the hundred and the check, when Talon crossed the George Washington Bridge into New Jersey.

54

"Idiots!" Bowles shouted. He was sitting in a dressing gown. The smell of a cheese soufflé lunch had replaced the odors of breakfast. "Idiots!" His study reverberated. The claws on the feet of his Chippendale desk practically dropped their clutched balls at the scream.

Charley already had his pants legs well pulled up and was sweating heavily. "That young southern guy on the pro team had it all together, sir—the phone trace-back and a positive I.D. by the room clerk. It was all perfect."

"Except it was all a setup!" The stentorian blasts were still coming. "This class-C clerk pulled everyone off base. Talon was stuck in New York, and now he's God knows where, doing God knows what!"

"Yes, sir."

"And on top of it all, the idiot you sent there shot some old tramp and damaged one of our own men."

"He was nervous, sir. But he would have killed Talon."

"Idiot! He didn't kill Talon; he killed a bum! The political ramifications of this are grotesque. We were set up."

"Yes, sir. We were."

Bowles's eyes rolled back in his head. His cool was escaping. The Ivy League aplomb was turning into bush-league panic. Charley kind of liked it.

"Get him," said Bowles. "He's like some V.C. in the jungle. Use everyone. Gas him. Bomb him. But get Talon!"

"I'll try, Mr. Bowles." Charley thought his boss might break down and cry, so he got up and left. He felt a minor victory over the patrician manipulators, but he had had nothing to do with it. Talon had done it. Talon was doing it. It was coming apart.

Get Talon, Bowles had said. Charley thought otherwise as he walked down the stairs of Bowles's tidy Georgian townhouse. First, he was going to clean out his safe-deposit box and buy a large briefcase. Then he was going to buy a ticket to Costa Rica, one-way. Then he was going to . . .

55

Greenbelt, Maryland. How many square miles in Maryland? Talon couldn't remember. Too many. Goddard Space Flight Center, the receiving station for Sanroc, is in Greenbelt. He had a plan, but he didn't know whether he had the time.

His head and ribs hurt as he pushed the scooter steadily

south at a sweet fifty-five on the Jersey Turnpike. The bike was pure, rolling honey. He kept the time with Carlee out of his mind by thinking of her before, not of what was left afterward.

The pounding his body was taking seemed unbearable. But he survived.

He drove into Baltimore a little after eight and checked into a motel. He took a long shower, washed out his socks and shorts, and hung them on the sink. He turned on the TV and watched Kojak suck lollipops and look cool. It was a different world. He couldn't remember the last time he'd looked at the tube.

He ached a lot. He thought about meditating, but couldn't hack it. He was too keyed up. So he went out, found a restaurant, and ate two rare steaks and a big green salad. The place didn't stock Foster's, so he settled for Bud. Then he went back to the motel.

He requested a wake-up call for five-thirty. He tried to sleep. His body needed rest, his head ached, and the wound on his side was making peculiar stains on the tape, but his mind raced with the wind. Soon it would be over. Soon he would rest. Soon.

56

Talon was already wide awake when the phone rang on Friday. The desk gave him a friendly good morning. He showered and shaved slowly, carefully. The moustache was looking less ratty. He prepared himself like Manolete, in the spirit of death in the afternoon.

At six-thirty he took off, doing a wheelie out of the parking lot. It hurt his body but sang to his soul. It was his middle finger to the real world, to "them."

He ran down the Baltimore–Washington Expressway, turned east on the Capital Beltway and north on 201. He turned right at Greenbelt Road and looked over the territory for a while. The day was clear and cool. Talon was loose and onstage.

He headed for the Capital core. He exited onto Route One from the Parkway and followed Rhode Island Avenue to Sixth Street. He ran fast in the early traffic. He stopped on Independence Avenue in front of the Department of Agriculture Building at eight-fifteen. He found a place to park the bike, hoped it wouldn't be towed or stolen, unfastened his paper bag, and started the process.

Talon flashed his plastic-encased identification card at the guard and was ushered in. Easy. After all, he could say "Hereford" and "mulch," and if the Company jockeys gave out the cards, why not use them?

He tried to get a handle on the situation when he got inside, doing his best to look as though he knew where he was going—no mean trick. Finally he stopped another early bird and asked him where the Landsat office was.

"The what?"

"Landsat—satellite surveys."

"Well, the survey department is on the second floor of the Annex."

"Thanks," said Talon.

He found the Annex and the Landsat department. He looked at his watch. Time was flying again.

There was a lady sitting there among a group of empty desks. She was reading the *Washington Post* and drinking coffee.

"Hi," said Talon.

She jumped out of her morning reverie and turned to him.

"Hello," she said.

"I'm from New York," he said, while leaning over the reception counter and flipping his wallet. She glowered at it, then back at him. Washington was full of birds, and he'd done his share of roosting during his training program.

"Yes?"

"I came down to check some Landsats. I wonder if you could set me up with a quiet spot and a viewer, darlin'." Manipulative bastard.

She looked interested but not persuaded.

Landsats are satellite computer photos that are not classified. They are used by government departments for agricultural, demographic, geological, and other scientific uses. He couldn't figure out what the hangup was.

"We're pretty crowded here. I don't know . . ." she said.

"It'll probably take less than an hour of scanning time, darlin'. And if your boyfriend won't have a myocardial infarction . . ."

"Huh?"

". . . heart attack, I will whisk you off to lunch tomorrow."

She looked at his drawn face and figured that with a little sleep he might be a good catch. She got up and walked to the counter. She smiled. "Silver-tongued devil. Let me see if I can find you a work space. Here's a request card. Why don't you fill it in while I look?"

"Right. Do you have an almanac?"

"Sure thing." She got one for him.

Other clerks started coming into the office. Talon leaned against the counter and turned to a perpetual calendar in *The World Almanac*. He spent some time counting back in nine-day increments—the Sanroc cycle. Then he filled in the dates of the prints he wanted. He looked up the capital-area quadrant in an index book and filled in the key numbers.

She came back and smiled possessively at him as another clerk offered to help. "He's mine," she said. The other clerk

182

blushed and scurried away. "I've got a work table and a 'scope for you, Mr. Talon. My name is Susan Stockwell. Need anything else?"

"Just a protractor and a ruler for now, Susan. The other thing we'll rap out later. Right?" He winked broadly at her.

"Sure thing, smooth talk." She glanced at the cards. "One in 1968 and a date last month. Prints of the D.C. area. Comparison?"

"Right." Nosy. He forced a smile.

"Come and sit. I'll get them for you." She went down a hall. He waited about twenty minutes until she came back with the two big Landsat prints and the tools of his trade.

"Thanks," he said and started to read them. She waited a few moments, shrugged and left.

Talon picked up the Goddard Space Flight Center in Greenbelt on both prints, and then worked his way out from there. With Goddard as the center, he drew ten concentric circles, each pair separated by one scale mile. Trying to make sense of the colors and blobs on the Landsats would have driven a layman crazy. To Talon, the 315-square-mile area he had bull's-eyed read like *Studs Lonigan*.

He got up and put the arm on Susan for a Magic Marker pen. Then he started scanning.

He was simply looking on last month's print for microwave dishes pointing to the sky. The override would have to use two of them. One of the dishes would be used to pick up the Sanroc telemetry signal and provide tracking for the second, which would broadcast the override information back to Sanroc at the appropriate time.

The 1968 Landsat photo had been made in the first year Landsat was flying, fully two years before Sanroc went into orbit. Therefore he could eliminate from suspicion anything resembling his target that showed up on both prints.

Intellectually the problem was not so complicated. If the override installation had been constructed after 1968, if

Ehrenzweig was right as to its location, if it existed at all, if Talon had enough time—if all those things worked, he might be able to spot the override base station in his comparison.

It took him until ten-thirty to finish up the later Landsat print. He had marked eighteen possibles. Of these, he eliminated twelve when he made the comparison with the early print.

By eleven-fifteen, he had eliminated two more after a careful second comparison. Four possibles. One was inside his first target area. The next was roughly west and at the far edge of his second one-mile ring. The last two were close together, north, and in the ninth-circle area. He tore the target area from the print, put a powerful fingerprint-identification microscope into his paper bag, and made for the door. No more time.

Susan Stockwell gave him a fish-eyed look as he trotted by, waving. He got on his bike. He exceeded prudent driving limits as he headed for Greenbelt. He stopped at a gas station on the way and paid fifty cents for a capital-area road map. He set up shop on the side of Greenbelt Road.

He zeroed in on the possibilities. The first was located in Berwyn Heights, a half-mile south of Greenbelt. He got there a little after twelve-thirty. The site was a private home. The roof was covered with antennas. He parked the bike and tried to be casual. A 1971 Buick was parked in the driveway. It had amateur radio call-letter plates and three whip antennas. He wrapped the Armalite rifle in the road map. The barrel and action were still stored in the plastic stock. He put the extra clip in his jacket pocket. He left the silencer and his toilet kit in the paper bag on the bike and hung the helmet on the handlebars.

From the Landsat print, the parabolic dishes looked to be to the rear of the house. Twelve-forty. He walked up the driveway to the side yard and tried to look over the high fence.

"Hey! You!"

Talon almost dropped his rifle. He felt stupid. This could be it. He turned to see a boy about seventeen. The boy was looking out from the kitchen doorway. "Yes?"

"What are you doing? I'm going to call a cop."

Not yet, thought Talon. Not yet. "Department of Agriculture. Soil research. Flood-plain study. I want to check the porosity of your soil."

"Huh?" The kid stepped out of the doorway and edged closer.

"I have to come back with the lab equipment. Your ham gear?" Talon pointed at the roof.

"My dad's."

Talon pulled out his wallet and flipped to his I.D. "Okay? I'd like to just check your backyard for a second to see if we can get our equipment in."

"My father's not going to like this. He hates government types. What's in the road map?"

"Present for my son. Quick peek?"

"Okay. C'mon." The kid unlocked the gate in the fence.

In a few seconds, Talon verified that there were two large microwave dishes on the ground in the backyard. Also, there was a clutter of other electronic gear. None of it was connected up to anything.

"Fine. Thanks," said Talon.

"Sure. Let me take your name and identification number, okay?"

"Right."

The kid already had a pencil out. More precious seconds gone.

57

Talon was back on his bike at a little after one. A mile and a half away, off Bucklodge Road, was the second site, in one of the huge tracts owned by the National Agricultural Research Center, adjacent to the University of Maryland. It lay to the northwest of Goddard. He arrived at the approximate location he had identified and scouted it carefully. The place was like a park—lots of trees and open spaces. He rode his bike up a hummock and looked around. He consulted the Landsat photo again and was sure he had to be at the right spot. Nothing. Just a power pole at the top of a nearby hill. He figured that might be something.

He pulled the bike onto its stand, carefully settling it so it wouldn't tip in the dirt. He walked to the pole. A dirt road ended there. A locked terminal box was set about eight feet up the pole. Some heavy tire tracks had made a big circle in the soil around the pole. There was a ten-by-fifty-foot concrete pad on the ground. One-twenty.

First he walked around the area. Nothing. Then he got on his bike and started to ride around in circles, pushing farther and farther away from the knoll. Nothing.

They must have moved it. If this was the spot. He was ready to pack it in and check on the two alternatives that were farther from Goddard, when he came across an old man who was puttering around with some seedlings. Talon stopped his bike, pulled off his helmet, and said hello.

"You're mucking up the place with that goddamn thing." He knelt there and looked sideways at Talon. He slapped at his Boss of the Road coveralls with a gnarled hand, then stood up and looked sour. He radiated the proprietary coolness of a baron confronting a poacher.

"Sorry. But I'm on urgent business."

"Must be."

"Yes, sir. I'm with Ag, too." Talon flipped out the handy I.D. for a quick flash. "There was some kind of van back there." He indicated the knoll.

"What's it to you?"

"I was supposed to pick up some research materials. That's where they said to go. I've got a rush job."

"Not much of an excuse. You should know better."

"I'm sorry, truly. But I got frantic. Can you help me?"

"I could."

"I'll get off your plants and out of your life."

"Faster, the better."

"Right."

"You're early. They set that van up there about once a week. . . ."

"Nine days?" Talon's heart started to pound.

"I suppose," he said. "Middle afternoon. It used to be there permanently, but there's been a lot of vandalism. You know how kids are. Anyway, about the last five or six months they've been dragging that big trailer up there. . . ."

"With the two parabolic reflectors on top?"

"Yes, if that's what they are. Anyway, they sit up there 'til late in the afternoon, I guess. It's gone the next morning."

"They've got three or four men in there?"

"Maybe inside. But all I ever saw was the driver. Then he goes inside, too."

"Thanks. More than I can tell you. I'm sorry about tracking on your land."

"No more, huh?"

"Right." Talon fired up, pulled the hat on and went straight back to Bucklodge Road. He found an unobtrusive place to put the bike, behind some trees near the unpaved side road. He took the Armalite rifle and wrapped it in the road map again. With the works stored in the plastic stock, it looked like part of a kid's toy. He put the silencer in his pocket. Then he took a deep breath to ease his shakes.

He walked up the dirt road. He was checking out the area around the power pole when he heard the sound of a vehicle laboring up the hill behind him. He walked quickly to some bushes about fifty yards from the pole. He looked around. He felt stupid, but he stretched out on the ground.

58

The truck that appeared was a tractor-trailer, decked out in the colors and logo of the Chesapeake and Potomac Telephone Company. The trailer had two microwave dishes on the top, mounted on tilting mechanisms. As Talon watched, the rig stopped next to the power pole, right on the concrete pad. The driver got out. He pulled off heavy cable from a reel at the side of the trailer. Then he scaled the pole, unlocked the terminal box, and plugged the cable in.

Talon checked his watch. Five after two. His hands were sweaty as he assembled his rifle and screwed on the silencer. Possession of that silencer is a Federal rap, he thought to himself. Screw 'em.

The driver opened a small box on the side of the trailer and worked some buttons. Hydraulic jacks at each corner of the trailer descended and raised the trailer until the driver was able to disconnect the fifth-wheel hitch from the tractor. He let the jacks raise the trailer until the wheels were clear of the ground. Then he adjusted the jacks, using a carpenter's level. He walked around the trailer. Apparently satisfied, he went to the back and unlocked the rear door. He climbed inside and shut the door.

Almost immediately, the two dishes started to rise on telescoping pylons until they were about twenty feet above the trailer roof. Then the dishes swiveled and turned down until they were pointed west, at the horizon.

Talon glanced at his watch. Two-twenty. Nothing was happening. He inserted a clip into the rifle and pulled the slide back. This was the part of the plan he didn't have together.

He was certain he was looking at the Sanroc override transceiver station. To protect it, they had murdered Carlee. He himself had been seriously injured. He was still being hunted. The people in there were parties to murder.

The pain associated with his discovery far outweighed any feelings of victory or elation. He waited and thought.

He thought about shooting out the power box. But they could have had a stand-by generator. He thought about shooting at the J-shaped tubular device set on the face of each of the parabolic antennas. These provided the pickup and transmission points for the signals. But the men inside could repair those, maybe, and they'd be tough to hit. The accuracy of his timing for disruption of the override became critical if it meant damaging something that could be repaired in short order.

As he watched, he saw the dishes lift slowly as the aligning signals from Sanroc were tuned in. In a few minutes, transmission would begin.

He got up from his hiding place and walked over to the trailer. Up close, he could hear the hum of fans and electronic equipment.

Murderers. He thought of his broken woman. He tapped the cylindrical fuel tank hanging under the tractor. He tried the cab doors. Locked, as was the fuel-filler cap. He stepped back and put seven shots into the tank, down low. The silencer worked well. The noise was just a string of coughs. He got out his pack of Kools and matches. He stooped down to light the fuel. But it was diesel. The match wouldn't light it.

He pulled the clip out and replaced it with his spare. He reloaded the first one. He aimed and shot at the sensitive mechanism that controlled the tilt of each of the big dishes on top of the truck, seven shots each. He sprinted back to the bushes and reloaded without looking at the trailer. He was so shaky that he could hardly get the little .22 long-rifle bullets into the clips.

He looked up in time to see one of the dishes start to move jerkily. Then he crawled about thirty feet to his right. He wanted a good view of the back of the trailer.

One of the rear doors swung open, and a man jumped out. He was wearing the same phone-company uniform as the driver. The guy looked up at the dishes and yelled something into the trailer. Then he started to climb up a ladder set into the side of the trailer. Talon aimed carefully. Seven more coughs. Smoke started to come from the terminal connection box.

The man on the ladder had heard the coughing. All of a sudden, the sounds of electrical and mechanical activity in the trailer died. The guy looked up at the dish mechanisms, then at the pole junction box, and put it together. He dropped down the ladder, ran in a crouch back around the trailer, and dove through the open rear door. A moment later, it slammed. Talon could hear the noise as a generator started up.

59

Mr. Bowles allowed his phone to ring four times before deigning to pick up the receiver.

"Hello."

"Hello, sir; this is Mark."

"Why are you calling direct? Where's Charles?"

"I'm in Charley's office, sir, and he's not here."

Bowles looked at the grandfather clock which dominated a corner of his study, with its seasons, phases of the moon, and solemn chimes. It had been his great-grandfather's. "It's nearly Sanroc time. Where the hell is he?"

"He hasn't been around today, sir. Anyway . . ."

"Find him!" Bowles felt an unfamiliar sinking sensation in his stomach. He reached for a bottle of Valium and a carafe of water.

"Yes, sir. Anyway, we've got a problem. The people at our translator site are taking fire."

Bowles tried to maintain calm. Charles must have gone over. Or . . . "Talon?" He poured some water in a glass.

"They don't know. But the dishes are dead, and they're using auxiliary power to transmit to us."

"They've only got about ten minutes," Bowles said. "They've got to get it going." His voice reflected the strain. The contagion spread.

"Yes, sir. I'll relay that. Then I'm leaving."

"Leaving? Hello?"

Mark had hung up on him. Bowles took two Valiums. Then two more. He started to consider the bottle of sleeping pills upstairs.

60

The shakes were wearing off. So was the adrenaline. Talon's energy level was rapidly decreasing. The pain from past abuse was pounding at him now. He held the little rifle, feeling exposed and alone. He wanted to run or walk. He had done all he could do.

The door of the trailer burst open, and two men hurtled out. They scuttled under the trailer and got behind the big tandem rear wheels, one man on each side. Talon rolled to his left, behind the crest of the knoll, to get broadside to the trailer. He crawled up to peer through the bushes. Now another man was going up the ladder. Talon edged the barrel of his rifle forward and put a couple of shots on the rungs. The guy dropped and rolled under the trailer.

"This side," he yelled, and immediately the air over Talon's head was filled with return fire and pieces of bushes. Bursts from an M-16 on full automatic echoed around the area, then a second joined in. They were sweeping the hill. They didn't have him yet.

Talon edged his face over the crest and saw two weapons poking out from behind the shelter of the double-bogie wheels on his side. The third man was on the ladder again. This time he was scanning the area. From higher up his angle was good. He spotted Talon almost immediately. Talon was already aiming when the guy yelled.

"Get him! Behind the bushes! Straight on!"

Talon squeezed off a few quick shots into the panel on the side of the trailer, the one that housed the controls for the hydraulic stilts for lifting and leveling the trailer. He gave up when bullets started kicking up the ground in front of him.

The trailer slowly settled down as the hydraulic system short-circuited and the jacks retracted. The men under the wheels had plenty of time to avoid the axle. The man on the ladder was hardly aware of any sinking sensation except the one in his guts. They had no chance of transmitting without a stable platform.

The man on the ladder jumped down and unlocked the tractor cab. He got in and started the engine. The trailer was now reunited with the tractor, the fifth-wheel pin in place. He made a sweeping turn and started back down the road. The gunners threw their weapons into the back of the trailer as it went by and jumped in after them. Talon wondered how far they'd get before the fuel quit. He watched it all before he passed out.

61

"Fancy piece of business, son."

Talon opened his eyes and saw the old man with the overalls standing above him, holding the Armalite rifle.

"You look like you're dying, but I didn't find any holes."

"I'm not in good shape."

"Sounded like a remake of World War II up here."

"A private war."

"You sure chased them away with this little thing." The old man cradled the gun and squatted next to Talon.

"I was the good guys."

"No such thing."

"I won. I think."

"Then you're the good guys."

"That all comes apart and fits in the stock. Except the silencer."

"This thing on the end?"

"Right. Don't get caught with it. Big Federal rap. Unscrew it."

"Make it yourself?"

"Right."

"Looks it."

The old man cracked some joints when he stood up. Then he plodded away, fondling the rifle.

Talon shook himself awake. He made it back to where the bike was hidden, part of the way on his hands and knees. He consulted his crumpled road map and pulled on the helmet. He started his bike and rode the fifteen miles to Walter Reed Hospital in a daze. He collapsed at the nurse's station as he pulled out his green Ag Department card.

62

On the following Tuesday, Tom Crest sat in his carrel in the Company's Sanroc analysis area at 26 Federal Plaza. He was musing over the increased security activity in the preceding ten days. He had been wired four times in that period, and there were a lot of goons from Langley milling around.

He was dedicated but unimaginative. However, it didn't take Joe Talon's mind to spot the cause of the aberrations on the second print he looked at. Area R201 had been remade by the N.R.O. computer just as Sanroc had picked it up. The first time ever. Crest lined up with two other analysts outside Jack Flynn's office that afternoon. They all had something important to say. And visions of promotions danced in their heads.

63

When Talon opened his eyes for the first time, he saw a blur in a white uniform move to his side.

"Where is this?"

"You're at the Walter Reed, Mr. Talon."

Female. Nurse. "Nurse?"

"Yes."

"What day?" He wished he had his contacts in.

"Wednesday. You've been here since last Friday."

"Condition?"

"Improving. You'd better check with the doctor on that."

He shook the I.V. in his arm.

"Don't do that."

"Right. I'm hungry."

"Check with the doctor . . ."

The rest of her sentence was lost as he went bye bye again.

64

"Talon, Talon, Talon . . ." A voice came out of the surf. The Lorelei calling him to his doom.

"Talon."

He opened his eyes and caught a couple of blurred forms hovering over him. He recognized Flynn's voice.

"What day?"

"Thursday, Joe."

"Who's with you? I don't have my eyes in."

"I'm from Langley," the voice said, "to observe."

Talon felt a surge of anger. He recognized Andy Alky's voice. "Get that drunken asshole out of here, M, or I swear I'll raise myself from the dead and do an act of kindness for the world." He started to flex his muscles and realized he was strapped to the bed.

"You'd better go," Flynn said to Blue.

"Look, I've got my orders. I observe the debriefing." Blue's insulation from the Bowery debacle and his report on Talon's missing print had increased his credibility and hence his self-esteem. He was a rock.

"You kidnapped and almost killed him," Flynn said. "Get out or I will bring criminal charges. I swear I'll see the Bureau."

"You wouldn't take the dirty linen out." Blue didn't sound too sure. It was almost a question.

"For you, I would."

"I'm going to call Langley on this, you bastard. And I'll get both him and you." He left.

"Thanks, M."

"You never stop getting my ass in a sling. Can we talk? You wouldn't believe the paper work."

"Debrief?"

"Yes."

"Hero or bum?"

"I guess that depends on to whom you talk. Some of both."

"Employed?"

"Want to stay?"

"I haven't thought about it. Where were the rats?"

"All over the place."

"Why?"

"Money. Mostly, in the beginning, it was patriotic. Like our other proprietaries—Air America, Southern Air Transport—the 'Delaware Corporations.' They provided us fat contracts, a big cash flow, and funding for operations that needed unappropriated, unknown dollars. The operations were shady, but people wanted them. Remember Chile? Anyway, after Vietnam, a lot of safe-deposit boxes got rented."

"The deal in Nepal was really big."

"Others, too. More than fifty million dollars a year. Probably the biggest wholesale dope operation in the world. Covered by their ground-station blackout of the real satellite images."

"The override."

"Yes, that's good. The override. More?"

"Go on. I'll live."

"Some small things. You forged a check on our account."

"Pay it. It was worth it, huh?"

"We did, but I'm not sure it was worth it."

"Get me the ownership for that scooter. Okay?" He thought about Carlee. "Get it for me. Promise?"

"Sure. Agriculture is getting sued for trespass. You did it."

"What?"

"Some guy has filed suit. You assaulted his son, tres-passed on his property, and spied on his radio equipment."

"The ham?"

"Yes, Joe."

"Pay him. The assault is bullshit. It was one of the possibilities."

"We will." Flynn started to shift around. He looked uncomfortable.

"What else, Jack? There's something else."

"Yes."

Blue marched back into the room triumphantly. "I've got orders to stay."

"All right," said Flynn. "We're almost done."

"What about them?" Talon said. "I don't blame you for being antsy. It went up to the top, right?"

"Not quite. It was a cabal in covert. Mostly middle management. They were financing some pretty sleazy activities."

"And themselves."

"And themselves. We have a high-level suicide, a talkative witness, some recent expatriates, and a bunch of lackeys in custody."

"The guys in the truck?"

"We've got all of them."

"How come no one picked up on the message I left in my carrel when this dingle let me escape?" He couldn't move his arms, so he angled his chin at Blue.

"You . . ." Blue started to heat up before he caught what Talon had said. ". . . what message?"

"I flagged the R201 print and your notes—big red X marks, dingle. Also, I left a computer sheet there with the key word on it. Ganja. Where's your redneck pal?"

"Cleaning toilets," Blue said absentmindedly. "You didn't snitch the print?"

"Not on your cheap-bar-scotch breath I didn't, dingle." He

tried for some strength, some timbre to his voice. It didn't work.

Blue was quiet. He closed his eyes and thought back to the morning after his run-in with the New York Police Department. He almost had it.

"What's happening?" said Flynn.

"Quiet, please," said Blue. Then he got it. "The cunt!" he said. "The cunt!"

"Huh?" said Talon.

"Who?" said Flynn.

"D'Arcy. She was in your carrel that morning, Talon. She cleaned it. She had a key. She was inside. That smartass southern politician was right, I'll give him that. He said either you"—he pointed at Flynn—"or the cunt was in it. One of you had to get the second safe-deposit key from the other to get Talon's carrel key."

"Oh," said Flynn. He started to get red.

"Excuse me," said Blue. "I gotta make a little history." He walked out.

Talon looked up at Flynn. He was tired. "I'm sorry, Jack."

"Yeah. I'm sorry for both of us. Me worse than you. They'll get it out of her. How the hell could I resist her? They took both of us. Shit."

"Me? How me?"

"Now?"

"Sure, now. After they hear you've been in the Company's pants, you'll be *persona non*." Talon was too hurt to be diplomatic.

"The girl you were with. She was one of ours. One of *theirs*."

"Carlee?"

"Was that the name?"

"Uh."

"She was covert. They'd had her with the last guy on your scan area, too. Backup, just in case. They always pushed us for single guys in that area; I never knew why. Beautiful, wasn't she? I've seen the photos."

"Uh."

"How did they know where you were when they ran you off the road?"

"I got a traffic ticket on the way out to Long Island. I guess they picked up on that." Talon tried to be hopeful. He wasn't very.

"Maybe. I figured she called in to report to them. We can check the long-distance calls from wherever you were and try to get a match-up with a Company number."

"Uh. Don't, huh?"

"They had her stored in a body bag at this guy Bowles's townhouse in Georgetown. In a freezer. He's gone, dead. The suicide. Her injuries told the story. Busted helmet, handbag, some extra clothes, all in there with her. We backtracked an address, keys, and some other stuff to you, Joe."

"Uh."

"I guess they figured you might come out after her. You think?"

"She was dead. After the accident."

"Maybe they figured you couldn't know for certain."

"Uh."

"And if you didn't, you'd come out. If you loved her, maybe. I don't know. If you had come out, you'd be cool meat now. Maybe they were going to show her to you. Shock treatment. Make a loose tongue. Could be she got hooked on you. For real. Maybe she just made the accident look more real. Anyway, she was excess baggage for some reason. Maybe they just couldn't wait to get you after your Saturday morning on the stolen computer terminal."

"But I didn't get anything. Not then."

"Close. You were pushing. Too close."

"Uh."

"Enough?"

200

"Uh."

"Good luck, Joe."

"Same to you, M."

"I'll try. Want anything, while I've still got a job?"

"My stereo, earphones and records. And the pink slip for my scooter? Don't forget."

"So long."

"Adios."

65

A bunch of horizontal hours went by for Talon. His body mended. The Beach Boys made a lot of sounds in his ears. The twisting in his gut over Carlee never stopped. Not for a minute.

A week after Talon talked with Flynn, Talon's new boss came in and they made some noises at each other. The people upstairs thought Talon was a big problem. A big pain in their collective Ivy League ass. An unemployable employee, but potentially more embarrassing on the outside. They were looking for something for him. That would take some time. Take off a couple of months with pay, Talon. Sure.

He walked out of Walter Reed early on a spring Saturday after four and a half weeks of healing, recuperation, and physical therapy. Blue brought him to his scooter with a minimum of verbal abuse, but only after Talon had signed a solemn oath to maintain secrecy.

Talon fastened down his toilet kit with the shock cords, made a mental note to pick up a sissy bar, and fired up. He didn't wave at the dingle. He didn't leave with a wheelie. He edged into traffic and pointed himself north. Heading home. The ache was still there, down deep. He rode all morning.

When he got near the Lincoln Tunnel exit, he pulled off the Jersey Turnpike into a service area. He got a number from information and dialed.

"It's me. Talon."

"Congratulations."

"On?"

"Being alive."

"You were right. It was there, near Greenbelt."

"Of course."

"Thanks for your help."

"You must tell me the whole story."

"Yes. I want to. And we can plan our trip."

"The surfing?"

"Yes, the surfing. Our deal. I have some time off."

"We can talk soon?"

"As soon as possible," Talon said.

"Anytime."

"Now?"

"Yes, Talon. You may come now."

"*Auf Wiedersehen.*"

"*Auf Wiederhören,* Talon."